The Man With The Tiny Head

Roger Longrigg

(Writing as Ivor Drummond)

HOUSE OF
STRATUS

This edition published in 2011 by House of Stratus, an imprint of Stratus Books Ltd., Lisandra House, Fore Street, Looe, Cornwall, PL13 1AD, UK.

www.houseofstratus.com

Typeset by House of Stratus.

A catalogue record for this book is available from the British Library and the Library of Congress.

ISBN 07551-0482-X
EAN 978-07551-0482-6

Prologue

The sun went down into the sea.

The little white clouds which the trade-winds carry unceasingly across the Caribbean – which hung now like a raggedy lace flounce along the horizon – turned rapidly from flame to purple to black. The strip of sea between the two dry, uninhabited little islands turned from yellow to blood to black. A young moon lay just over the tangled trees of the larger island. The sky was immediately full of stars. The wind dropped to a whisper. Tiny, irritating insects came out of crannies and drifted over the dark beaches: but there was no one for them to sting, no one for miles.

Some prehistoric electricity was switched on among the vicious, inhospitable, useless vegetation of the two little islands – among the mangroves and sea-grapes and dusty cactus – and suddenly all the tree-frogs began to bong over the quiet water, *bleep-bloop, bleep-bloop,* an interminable electronic music, monotonous, magical. The noise of the cicadas, like a million tiny bicycles, chirred under the song of the frogs.

At the edge of the water, on the wet volcanic rocks and the dead coral, sea-snails with conical shells twitched and slithered. In the water, creatures with feelers and teeth and spikes and spines and poison waited, with endless patience, for the chance to kill each other.

A rhythmic thudding became dimly audible. It grew very slowly louder. A diesel motor, throttled right back. A yacht? But no yacht navigates for choice among the islands at night – it is dangerous: it is unnecessary.

Yes, a yacht, visible now in the channel between the islands (but there was no one to see it) – a big boat, a ketch, white-hulled in the moonlight, sails furled, inching along the narrows. No navigation lights, no lights on deck, no lights showing through the portholes or the windows of the saloon. No sound except the muffled thud of the diesel.

The timbre of the engine changed. The yacht stopped moving, the anchor-chain went down with a roar and the anchor splashed. The engine cut.

Still no light from the yacht. Now no sound except for the frogs and crickets to whom a yacht, more or less, was a matter of indifference. Little tired ripples from the yacht's screw and her hull and the dropping of her anchor sucked at the beaches and died under the starlight.

'Mr *Warren*,' said the slim man in the pink shirt, bouncing down the steps from the cockpit into the big saloon, 'Mr *Warren*, you're not *drinking!*'

The fat, fiftyish American raised his head from his hands. It was true that the glass in front of him was empty. So also was the bottle. His eyes swivelled and his mouth hung open.

'Not drinking?' he finally said. His voice was blurred and uncertain and a long way away, like an announcer on a badly tuned radio. 'I have been.' He laughed, as though scoring a debating point of uncommon shrewdness. 'I have been drinking, George.'

'*And* will again. *And* will again. We *got* here! It's *party* time!'

The big man looked round the saloon. He was sitting on a long, blue-cushioned seat; another faced him, with a shiny table between. There were also basket chairs, and low chairs of aluminium and plastic; a wall-vase with an arrangement of bougainvillaea; a bamboo magazine-rack full of copies of *Playboy*; yacht photographs on the walls. There were heavy, impenetrable curtains over the ports. It was not one of the cramped and functional saloons of small yachts and ocean racers: nor was it distinctive in any way. It was exactly like the saloon of nearly every other expensive charter-yacht in the Caribbean. Except that there were no people. There was no party.

'No party,' said Mr Warren with grief. He shook his head slowly. The heavy flesh between jawbone and collarbone wobbled as he moved. His lower lip wobbled damply. 'Where's girl? Where's lil girl?'

'She'll be right *up*,' cried George with glee. The thin face and arms that stuck out of George's pink shirt were so deeply tanned that his original colouring was impossible to guess. His smile was wide and bright, and his dark hair waved prettily. He looked as queer as a coot.

He tripped to a door at the after end of the saloon and opened it. It gave on to a short companionway into a cabin. 'Caroline,' he called. 'Caroline, honey. Come join the *party,* dear.'

A man appeared at the foot of the steps. 'She'll be right up. She's all ready.'

'Cooking nicely, Lyn?'

'On the boil, George.'

Lyn's tan matched George's. He was so brown he was almost blue. His hair was fair and he wore very tight white cotton pants and his shirt was made of somebody's yellow bath-towel.

George shifted a cushion, lifted the lid of a locker and pulled out another bottle of Johnny Walker. 'New bottles for *old,* Mr Warren.' He poured a stiff drink and dropped three ice-cubes into it, delicately, clucking when a little splash threw a drop of whisky on to the table. 'Excuse *fingers,* please.'

'You not drinking, George? Hey? Where's party?'

'*Sure* I'm drinking, and so is *Lyn,* and so is *Caroline.*'

He poured himself a very long weak drink and raised his glass with *bonhomie.* Mr Warren raised his glass too, since it was clear that the party had begun. Mr Warren took a long pull of his own big strong drink.

Lyn appeared in the doorway, gently pushing a girl.

'Here they *are*,' said George. 'Who's *drinking?*'

Mr Warren looked at the girl. The point of his tongue appeared and very quickly licked his upper lip and then his lower lip, and he drank some more of his drink. He fumbled for a cigarette from the pack in the breast pocket of his shirt. George was very quick with a tiny jade-green lighter with a design of mignonettes. Mr Warren went on looking at the girl.

Caroline was very young and very juicy. A pink-and-white girl, gold from cautious exposure to the sun. She was certainly not more than eighteen, and probably not less than sixteen.

(But it is no longer easy to be sure, these days.)

She had long, straight fair hair and big blue eyes and there was no expression in her face at all. Her mouth was a little open, like Mr Warren's. It was much prettier than Mr Warren's. She was a very pretty girl indeed. She did not look a clever girl – indeed, at the moment, she looked moronic – but she was very pretty. Her legs were good, golden, well-rounded, visible to high-mid-thigh under a wild-coloured cotton shift. Her bare arms were golden and rounded: hanging limply now, but imaginable in many useful and vigorous activities. Her shift hung from juicy shoulders by narrow straps, one of which was waywardly slipping over the point of its shoulder. The edge of her golden tan was visible. The untanned upper hemisphere of her breast was smooth and white as a china soup-plate.

Mr Warren's tongue very quickly licked his upper lip and then his lower lip, and he took a drag at his cigarette. Without taking his eyes from the girl he raised his glass. It was empty. George, watchful, nipped forward and filled it, and put three lumps of ice delicately in after the whisky.

'Excuse *fingers*.'

There was no definite evidence that Caroline was wearing anything under her shift; there was, on the contrary, some evidence that she was not.

'Where you been?' said Mr Warren huskily.

'Me?' said the girl unexpectedly, in a high clear voice.

'Where you been?'

'Caroline's been resting up so's to be right in shape for the party,' said George. 'Right, Lyn?'

'Right, George,' said Lyn. 'Right, Caroline?'

'Absolutely right,' said Caroline. Her voice sent a shiver through Mr Warren. It was the unmistakable, arrogant, be-damned-to-you voice of the English upper classes. High and light, a schoolgirl's voice, the assured and very young voice of a girl at a very expensive English school.

Her feet were bare, like Lyn's and George's. Mr Warren wore white leather loafers. Mr Warren was very red from the sun; you could assume he was visiting the Caribbean from some cooler and dimmer climate. You could assume, from his face and clothes and manner (drunk as he was) that he was rich and important. He smelled of money and authority. Through his mumbling you could glimpse the rigid and ingrained selfishness of the powerful.

'Sit right here, Caroline,' said Mr Warren.

Caroline sat right there, beside him on the seat George darted forward with a full glass for Caroline. It was medium strength, between the dark brown of Mr Warren's drink and the pale straw of his own and Lyn's.

Caroline's eyes were made up, not skilfully. There was no make-up on her face or her lips. She was slightly shining with sweat – all her face and her arms and her golden thighs as she sat by Mr Warren, and the white of her breast below the edge of her tan, all her flesh was damp with a slight sheen of sweat. She drank her drink and smoked a cigarette without inhaling, and presently Mr Warren put his hand on her thigh.

She turned to face him, her mouth open, her big blue eyes half closed. Mr Warren put his hand under her wayward shoulder-strap. Mr Warren kissed her. Mr Warren began to take liberties with Caroline's dress and her person.

George caught Lyn's eye, then eased up out of the saloon into the cockpit. Lyn slipped quietly out by a door at the forward end of the saloon. On his way he pressed two switches with the effect not (as might have been expected under these romantic circumstances) of leaving a dimmer light, but on the contrary a much more brilliant light over the two long seats. He closed the door softly behind him.

Forward of the saloon was the galley. Bolted to the metalwork of the cooker was a 16-mm movie-camera, its lens probing through a hole in the forward wall of the saloon. A pale untidy man with a blue chin and thinning hair was operating the movie-camera, which made very little sound and which could swivel and tilt freely without any sound.

'They're in shot, Julie?' whispered Lyn.

'They'll be centre-screen. Hey, see that? Hey, this guy is a fast worker.'

'You envy him, Julie?'

'Certainly I envy him. Even though it's rape.'

'It is not rape! Look at her! Jesus, look at her! How can you say this is rape?'

'Virtually it is rape. Certainly I envy him.'

'Make a good movie, Julie, will you? You get it all.'

'What I do for money.'

Julie kept his eye to the viewfinder. He swung the camera a little and twitched the focus. His balding head was covered with big drops of sweat.

'Photography,' he murmured. 'Making pictures. I been crazy about pictures since I was in school. My ambition, always my one single ambition was to get to be the guy behind the camera.'

'So here you are,' said Lyn. 'Small-town boy makes good.'

'98th Street boy makes blue movies.'

'We all got to live.'

'My sister got to live. Third operation coming up.'

'Tough.' Lyn lowered his eye to a peephole. 'That's my baby, Mr Warren. Keep at it, kid. You know something, Julie? You're right. This time it is rape.'

'Sure it's rape, the lucky bastard.'

Lyn was sweating now, too, in the close air of the galley. George in the comparative cool of the cockpit was barely damp. Caroline was drenched in sweat. Her gay little shift was now an untidy bandage round her waist; otherwise she was naked and slippery, and a little of her was very white and soaking wet and much of her was golden and soaking wet. She was weakly pushing at Mr Warren and fighting him and trying to push him off, but he was lying on top of her now and had taken off his own clothes and he was strong and heavy and not full of dope. He was sweating too and his expensively cut grey hair was wet and he was breathing harshly through his mouth and raping Caroline.

Caroline moaned but was unable to scream. Mr Warren put a big hand over her nose and mouth in case she screamed.

There were rings of moisture on the table from their drinks, and Mr Warren's last cigarette had rolled out of the ashtray and burned a long black furrow into the shiny table.

The movie-camera hummed, hardly audible over the hum of the icebox in the galley.

Caroline stopped struggling and everything was easier for Mr Warren. He kept his hand over her mouth in case she screamed. Presently he lay on top of her, panting. Then he took his hand from her face and withdrew from her and looked blearily round the saloon. Caroline's head lolled sideways and her mouth was open. Her arms were limp and she lay flat on her back and the whites of her eyes were showing.

'She's out cold,' whispered Julie. His shirt stuck to his back and the camera hummed.

Mr Warren reached for his clothes and started to pull them on. He found it difficult to dress. He tried to pull Caroline's skirt down, but it was rolled up and soaking with sweat and it was too difficult for him.

'Come on, baby,' he said thickly. 'How do you feel? Come on, how about it, wake up, will you?'

'You know what I think?' whispered Julie. 'I think that kid is not good.'

'She's a good kid,' said Lyn, who was not really interested in Caroline and who had turned away from the peephole and lit a cigarette.

'She's still out cold. She looks bad. You ought to do something.'

'Wait till uncle's dressed. We don't want to embarrass him.'

Soon Mr Warren was decent, if not dapper. Caroline had not moved and was not decent.

Lyn came back into the saloon. At the same time George came down from the cockpit, arriving with the little leap used by people who want to show they are athletic in a confined space.

George made Mr Warren another drink. Lyn tried to wake Caroline up. After a few moments it occurred to him that she was dead, and it was immediately clear that this was so.

Lyn showed some disposition to panic. 'Jesus, what we do? Jesus, what we do? Jesus, what we do?'

'Lash her to the spare anchor and sink her under the west cliffs where it's real deep. Don't *fret,* Lyn. You didn't do it.'

'I didn't, did I?' said Lyn, brightening.

'Mr Warren did it.'

'He did, didn't he?'

'He *did* it, by his *lone*some, nobody else was even *in* here.'

'But his secret is safe with us.'

'Safe as Fort Knox.'

'And he'll need Fort Knox, all the gold in the world,' said Lyn, quite cheered up. 'And the boss won't be mad at us?'

'I can't think why he *should,* Lyn. Mr Warren was all alone with Caroline. *Check,* Mr Warren?'

'Check, Mr Warren?' said Lyn gaily.

But Mr Warren had once again buried his face in his hands, and it was doubtful if he was aware of anything going on round him.

'I don't believe he took it in,' said George with gentle sympathy. 'What a shock it will be, Lyn.'

Julie came into the salon, carrying the camera which he had

unbolted from the galley.

'Cut these lights, Julie, please', said George. 'No point in *waste.*'

'This time is one time too much,' said Julie flatly. 'And I want plenty of light.' 'Don't *fret,"* said George. 'Mr Warren had a little accident. It isn't any business of ours.'

'It's between Mr Warren and his conscience,' said Lyn primly. 'Who are we to judge?'

'You lousy little fairies,' said Julie. 'I shoot these stinking movies, okay, I need the dough and I don't give a goddam what you do with them. But this time is one time too much.'

'You know, Lyn,' said George, 'maybe after all the boss could get a little mad. He trusted us to find a guy who could get the pictures without fail and keep quiet without fail. Will you keep quiet without fail, Julie?'

'I got a conscience too,' said Julie. He looked down at the pathetic damp empty flesh on the seat, with the damp roll of bright fabric pathetically round its waist.

'And you got a sister, and her third operation coming up,' said Lyn.

'Tough,' said George. 'It's a hard old world, Julie.'

'Not that hard,' said Julie.

Julie looked from George to Lyn and back to George and his expression was glum and determined.

'This kind of talk makes me nervous,' said Lyn, who did not look nervous.

'Don't fret.'

'Remember what the boss said about bad security risks?'

'Yes, *indeed.* I know exactly what the boss would want we should do.'

George turned to a chart-table and opened a drawer. Keeping his body between Julie and the drawer he took out an automatic pistol and screwed a silencer to its muzzle.

'Got the film, Julie?' he asked over his shoulder.

Julie shrugged. 'In the camera.'

'Good boy.'

George turned and shot Julie in the chest. Lyn caught him and they carried him quickly up on deck. There was almost no blood on the saloon floor; Lyn sponged up what little there was with a damp cloth from the galley. He rinsed the cloth and hung it up neatly, as though he enjoyed housework and liked a nice clean home.

Mr Warren was aware of the dull plops of the silenced gun, which were quite loud in the saloon. He looked round and drank from his drink.

'We got two spare anchors?' asked Lyn.

'No. We'll sink Julie with a few yards of chain.'

They picked up Caroline and laid her on the afterdeck beside Julie.

'I'll get the chain,' said Lyn.

'Change your *pants* first, Lyn. You'll get all dirty.'

'Sure.'

Lyn went below. As he passed Mr Warren, Mr Warren focused on him and said: 'How's girl?' He said it a second time, carefully, concentrating on clarity: 'How is the girl?'

'Be fine, Mr Warren. Over-excited, I guess, maybe a drink too many. Getting a little fresh air. Be fine.'

'Okay.'

Mr Warren lay down, exactly where Caroline had lain, and fell gustily asleep.

George started the diesel, raised the anchor with the power winch, clicked into forward gear at very low revs and steered slowly and carefully out of the narrows. He knew the place well and it was easy to see by moonlight and starlight. On a dark night, and for a stranger, it would have been dangerous.

Lyn came up on deck in picturesquely tattered jeans. He got the chain and the spare anchor from their lockers, and lashed the two corpses to them. He joined George in the cockpit and adopted a pose which emphasised the slimness of his hips.

'So now we're fresh out of help,' said Lyn.

'No problem. Oily Feld can find us a photog in New York. And the boys in London can ship us another piece of aristocratic ass. We'll cable first thing.'

'The boss is in Britain right now.'

'Sure, so he is. Inspecting the machinery. So now he can really see it operate.'

'Will he like that?'

'*Sure* he'll like it. And he wouldn't want we should wait around not earning.'

'He would not, George. He would not.'

When the yacht was clear of the islands the motor changed to a higher and louder note, and they were travelling away at eight knots. The noise of the engine soon became inaudible under the monotonous electronic *bleep-bloop, bleep-bloop* of the tree-frogs and the chirring of the cicadas. Little waves from the yacht snaked over the smooth water and rustled among the sea-snails and the conches and the roots of the mangrove trees.

1

February in London.

The streets of Soho were choked in a freezing fog. Maltese, Cypriots, Italians, Greeks and Chinese coughed behind scarves. The walls of buildings looked as though they had been coated in cold grease. The people looked as though they had been dug up.

It was one o'clock: lunchtime. But the day seemed either not to have got properly light in the morning, or already to have started to get dark in the evening.

A row of restaurants emitted a welcoming glow, and none more than the *Paese,* which had hams and cheeses and china fruit in its window.

A big man in a coat with a fur collar walked fast along the street. He was bareheaded; his hair was dark and curly. He stopped in front of the *Paese* and pushed open the door. He looked as though he could equally easily have pushed a hole through the wall. In his big brown hand the door handle looked like a thimble.

The restaurant was crowded and quite noisy. There was a smell of onions and garlic and hot fat.

A little man in a black coat looked up when the door opened. He saw brilliant blue eyes in a big ugly brown face, and he ran to the door.

'*Signor conte! Che felicità!*'

'*Buon giornio, Emilio. Come sta?*'

Il Conte Alessandro di Ganzarello (23rd of his line) shook hands with the little manager. In his hand the manager's hand looked like the white hand of a doll.

Emilio opened a door behind a grubby red curtain. There was a staircase immediately behind the door. *Il conte* went up, taking off his coat as he went. Under the coat were a dark blue suit, unmistakably English and a white silk shirt, unmistakably Italian.

He opened another door at the top of the stairs, and he was in the *Paese's* private room. There were some bad, romantic paintings of the Italian lakes; otherwise the decor was much like that of the restaurant below – dark wood, fringed lampshades, a checked tablecloth.

Drinks were set out on the sideboard. The table was laid for three.

Il conte went to the sideboard and poured himself a Campari and soda. He then inspected the pictures with a look of disgust. He took the most lurid off its hook with his free hand and hung it up again with its face to the wall. It was a big picture, massively framed; he lifted it with one hand as though it were a postcard.

There was an armchair near the sideboard. *Il conte* lowered himself into it and stretched out his legs. The effect was of a steel spring gently uncoiling but likely at any moment to coil up again and become a powerful machine.

He was forty-five. There was a little grey in his hair.

Light footsteps could be heard running up the stairs. The man began to smile. The door opened explosively, swinging round so that it bashed the wall beside it. A girl came in.

All that could at first be seen of her was a very shaggy short coat made from the skin of some unidentifiable longhaired beast. Below the coat were long and perfect legs. There was a gleam of very bright fair hair above the coat.

The girl took the coat off and dropped it on the floor. It lay looking like an animal recently shot.

She was wearing a tight yellow dress with a short flared skirt. Her figure was superb, to match her legs. Her face was not so much beautiful as breathtakingly pretty. It was round and innocent and charmingly asymmetrical – she showed, when she smiled, a deep dimple in one cheek only.

She smiled now and ran across the room with her arms held out. The Italian was standing up. He embraced her. 'Ciao, carina.'

'Sandro, love!'

'How did it go, Jenny?'

'Messy but all right.'

'Have one drink and tell me quickly.'

'Why only one?' As she poured Glenlivet whisky Jenny said: 'We nabbed all four of your nasty little Greeks at their nasty little farmhouse. They'd just taken delivery, as you said. Their pockets were bulging with heroin.'

'Don't tell me they came quietly.'

'No. But only one's dead.'

'You shot him?'

'Well yes, I rather had to, I do dislike it so.'

'I also, usually, but not drug-traders on that scale. So I have closed the beginning of the pipeline and now you have closed this end of the pipeline.'

'Sickening for them.'

'They were the most efficient and dangerous group in Europe,' said Sandro seriously. 'I wish they were all dead.'

'Some of yours are, surely.'

'Certainly. Some we fortunately killed, out on the sea.'

'Do the Italian police know about that?'

'Not in detail. In any case they feel moral indignation about the drug traffic. Where is Colly? He must by now have told them in New York.'

'Pop a cork and I bet he comes running.'

'Jenny . . . '

'Yes, darling?' 'This job is finished.'

'Yes, such a relief. I've never been so bored or so frightened.'

'I also. Now I must probably go home for a little.'

'And Colly, to all his yachts and clubs and whisky. *Sickening* your both rushing off. We never seem to see each other nowadays except when we're busy.'

'Just exactly so. For that exact reason I suggest a different arrangement.'

He embraced her gently. The effect was of a huge and benevolent bear embracing a humming-bird.

'Oh, Sandro pet.'

'I will love you till I die.'

'Darling, me too, you know that.'

'It is such a nuisance that I am married.'

'Flavia seems quite clear you're divorced. So does her husband.'

'He is not her husband. They are deluded. There is no such thing as divorce. The arrangement which I suggest . . . '

Jenny put her fingertip in the deep cleft of his chin and pushed his face away gently and looked at him. The big, ugly, attractive face with the blazing blue eyes looked back at her, smiling. She knew that many women had loved Sandro very much, and she knew why, and she knew that it was true that he loved her. She also knew that these attempts he made, always at the end of a job, were a mixture of habit and politeness.

'I yearn for what you have in mind, pet, but just at the moment another drink is what I most need.'

Sandro laughed and let her go.

'Besides, darling, I love Colly.'

'I know, more,' said Sandro with a pretence of angry tragedy.

'Just the same. How did your morning go?'

'We got the little men.'

'All?'

'Eighteen. No, not all. The police were quite good.'

More footsteps could be heard climbing the stairs. They were irregular and shuffling. They were the footsteps of someone either pitiably infirm or else extraordinarily lazy.

The door opened slowly. A man in his early thirties stood

15

leaning against the doorpost. He seemed in the last stages of exhaustion. He was medium-sized, with mouse-coloured hair and greenish eyes; he wore a sort of tank-coat, a garment without distinction.

'Colly, darling!' said Jenny.

'Hi, kids,' said Colly. He came into the room as though his feet hurt and his legs were unbearably tired. 'Those stairs.'

He and Jenny kissed and he grinned at Sandro.

'The entire New York police force will at this minute be running around hitting people on the head with clubs.'

'Hard, I hope.'

'Pretty goddam hard. The Commissioner was whistling like a kettle. Sizzling. I could practically smell burning right along the transatlantic cable.' Colly sank into the armchair and closed his eyes. 'Give me a shot of that Scotch, will you, darling? I had a very, very exhausting time with the telephone.'

'Get it yourself, you slob,' said Jenny. Nevertheless she made and handed him a drink.

'Now where is our lunch?' said Sandro. He went to the door and shouted: 'Emilio!'

The bottom door opened and Emilio looked up. They had an intense and protracted conversation in Italian about the cooking of the veal.

'I'll have to get back pretty soon,' said Colly quietly to Jenny.

'I know. Miserable.'

'Thought I'd sail *Perelandra* down to Grenada or some place.'

'Hard work.'

'Hell, I don't pull on any ropes. Jenny, listen.' Colly's voice suddenly became serious. 'Come with me. Give up that screwy job.'

'Oh, I will, in a day or two. I only did it for a cover.'

'Come sail *Perelartdra* down to Grenada. It's almost a full moon. Sea's in the eighties. I want you on your own.'

'Wouldn't it be bliss?'

'I love you, Jenny.'

'I know, darling. I love you too.'

'I know it. Come.'

Jenny smiled at him. Coleridge Tucker III, idler, multimillionaire, always apparently too tired to push one foot in front of another. Tanned, unremarkable face, loose-jointed average body. Unfailing good nature, unvarying lethargy. People in New York said it was an appalling waste. Many girls said they would have loved him if only he got around to coming alive. Jenny knew exactly what they meant. And she knew Colly with the mask off, Colly out from under the habitual, impenetrable camouflage – Colly swift and decisive and frightening.

'If I didn't love Sandro so much, darling, I really almost might.'

'How is it,' said Colly, 'that you tease and tease and tease the both of us to hell and gone, and yet you're not a tease? And how is it they let you drink Scotch when you're only fourteen years old?'

'I say I'm fifteen,' said Jenny.

Sandro won his argument with Emilio and they were soon eating.

'I must say I pine for a rest,' said Jenny.

'Most important,' said Sandro.

'And then what, I wonder?'

'Somebody or something will come plucking at our sleeves,' said Colly.

'Please everybody,' said Jenny, as though addressing the world, 'stay out of trouble for a month.'

A nasty day turned into a nasty evening.

Jenny, her long bright hair almost hidden by her shaggy coat, scampered to her Mini in the street outside her flat. It was time she went to work.

The fog was patchy at Hyde Park Corner but it grew thicker near the river. There were few other vehicles on the streets. The lights had misty haloes. The Mini's heater roared and the windows steamed up.

Jenny drove down Sloane Street and along the King's Road. Dark shop-fronts, a greasy surface, no pedestrians.

She passed a stationary taxi, and in front of it two men pushing a car. She slowed down. You couldn't leave people stranded on an evening like this. She stopped and began to get out of the Mini.

The crippled car was a battered little grey two-seater. A burly, muffled figure was at the wheel. The engine fired and the driver revved hard. It sounded healthy. The noise was loud in the quiet foggy street. Jenny expected the car to stop. But it accelerated away, past her, down the King's Road and out of sight.

'Well, I'm damned,' said one of the men who had been pushing. 'The bugger never even stopped to say thank you.'

Jenny knew the voice. An ordinary, nice, well-scrubbed, ambitious upper-middle-class young man, rendered more interesting in recent weeks by a fascinating new girl-friend. 'Nigel, love,' she called, 'were you hoping for a tip?'

'This evening,' said the other man, 'has got off to a lousy bloody start.'

Jenny went up to them.

'Hullo, Jenny,' said Nigel. He was about thirty, conventionally dressed in brown felt hat and dark overcoat. He looked vexed. 'Foul man covered in ginger whiskers. Flags our cab down, asks for a push, we push his filthy car, and the sod just speeds off.'

'Lousy bloody start,' said the other man.

'Do you know each other? My boss, Dave Maddox, Jennifer Norrington.'

Nigel's boss was fortyish, very smooth, in a camel-hair coat and a Paisley scarf. Jenny remembered that Nigel was in advertising; this certainly looked like an advertising boss.

'We're going to your nosh-house,' said Nigel.

'Good,' said Jenny. 'I'll give you a special bottle after your pushing. Just the two of you?'

'No, no. Girls in the cab.'

Nigel indicated the taxi thirty yards away. An old taxi, the driver apparently bowed with age and muffled like an Eskimo. The taxi crunched into gear and began to move towards them.

'Picking us up,' said Camel-hair with approval.

But the taxi suddenly turned left and thudded up a side-street.

'What the hell?'

'Jokes,' said Jenny. 'Have you got Nicola?'

'Yes,' said Nigel. 'Yes, of course.'

'There you are. She's a great one for jokes.'

'I'm not madly amused, quite frankly,' said Camel-hair. 'Your bloody Nicola is not improving her prospects in the company.'

Nicola was Nigel's new girl, the one who had made him more interesting, the one who might jolt him out of his dreary middle-class ambitions and make him into someone Jenny could respect. (Jenny was aware that her views on such subjects were not the usual ones. To her the things most people seemed to want for themselves spelt a living death: while the things she thought they ought to want would have sent them, scuttling and terrified, into bombproof rabbit-holes.) Nicola was eminently capable of jokes like this disappearance.

'Nicola works for you too?' she said to Camel-hair with surprise.

'For your friend Nigel. He took her on.'

'Ah,' said Jenny, understanding. To her there could be no better reason for hiring someone at a thumping salary than the fact that you fancied them.

'She's exceedingly intelligent,' said Nigel defensively.

'I know *that*, pet.'

'Let's get a move on in *some* direction *some* time,' said Camel-hair crossly.

'I'll give you a lift,' said Jenny. She saw the man's point. It was very unpleasant standing about in the street. 'It's only a medium spit from here, anyway.'

She drove them to The Joint and they scrambled out.

'This place better be good,' said Camel-hair, who seemed to

Jenny a spoilt and ill-tempered man.

They advanced towards the restaurant. The 'J' of Joint, on the sign over the door, was wittily formed of a naked female leg terminating at the top in a well-rounded buttock. Camel-hair stared at this conceit.

'Three joints,' he finally said.

'Mm?' said Jenny, locking her Mini.

'Arse-knee-ankle. Cute idea. Can't we pinch it for something, Nigel?'

'Which do you want to pinch,' said Nigel, 'arse, knee or ankle?'

Camel-hair laughed. This was evidently his sort of joke, which was evidently why Nigel had made it. Good humour restored, the three of them went down the narrow stairs into the restaurant.

The joint was large, dark, crowded, noisy and gay. The customers were young and minor theatrical figures, journalists, a few advertising men, two television personal aides and some girls on the make. The waitresses were out-of-work actresses and the manager was an ex-actor.

'They're probably here,' said Jenny, 'waiting for you and giggling girlishly.'

'Can't see them.'

The manager came up. 'Jenny! Once again *intolerably* late.'

'Darling, I cringe. I've been rescuing the shipwrecked. Have two girls just arrived?'

'I expect so, indeed. Those two?'

Not those two. Those three in the corner? No, for God's sake. That one? No, she'd been waiting for an hour.

'That's funny,' said Nigel.

'Maybe,' said the manager, 'they got tired or someone picked them up or they stopped for a drink.'

He was not interested. Parties frequently fragmented on their way from bars or flats or theatres. Sometimes they reformed, sometimes not. Every evening produced a few disgruntled gentlemen dining alone and a woebegone girl or two drinking coffee or Coke.

'Table for two?' said the manager.

'They'll turn up in a minute. We'll have a drink meanwhile.'

'If they're peckish they'll come,' said Jenny. 'I must speed off and change and get to work.'

Time passed.

'Could the taxi have broken down?' wondered Nigel aloud. 'Got lost in the fog? Accident?'

'Joke, eh? You can tell Miss Nicola Bland from m e . . . '

Camel-hair, now Pin-stripe, seemed to think it unnecessary to finish his message. He was right. His tone told all.

'I don't know,' he went on presently, 'if that other bird, that Tamara, would have been much of a gas, anyway.'

'Beautiful girl,' said Nigel.

'Dull. Little model from Lewisham. Probably virtuous. Don't see her opening her legs, quite frankly. But I'm still bloody annoyed at not getting the chance to find out.'

'What in hell,' wondered Nigel for the hundredth time, 'can have happened to them?'

They finally decided to eat. The wine-waitress brought the wine list. The wine-waitress was Jenny.

The eyes of Nigel's boss, busy with thighs all evening, popped at the sight of her. It was not only that she was the prettiest girl of all the pretty girls in the room. It was also her garb that visibly impressed him. She now wore a long, loose Shetland sweater which just covered whatever pants she had on; she had sandals on her feet; between sandals and sweater her legs were bare.

'Still no girls?' she said.

'We can't think what's happened.'

'*Sickening* for you. It happens all the time. What are you eating?'

She took their order and trotted away. Nigel's boss turned all the way round to watch her. He wondered if she *was* wearing pants. Nigel assured him that, as far as he knew, she always did.

'She's rather a sweetie, don't you think? Quite dotty. The whole family's barking. She says that's the best way to dress in her job, because you can squeeze between the people so easily.'

'*Squeeze* . . . it's a funny job for a girl like her to have.'

'She has a million jobs for about ten days each. She's been here six weeks, it's a record. She sold flowers for a bit—'

'In the *street?*'

'No, no, a grand shop. That was only three days. Then she popped up as a secretary in one of the film companies—'

'She doesn't look like a secretary.'

'She's not. She did her shorthand in longhand and typed with two fingers. It took them three weeks to find out. She's quite dotty.'

Jenny brought them their claret. 'What a *long* joke,' she said to Nigel, who looked crestfallen. 'Have you rung up her flat?'

'Oh. No. Should I? Yes, I ought to have thought of it.'

He came back saying: 'No reply.'

'Should you go round there?'

'Yes. No. If she was there she'd answer the telephone. Unless she's been . . .'

'What?'

'Unless she's gone fast asleep or something. In which case there'd be no point in standing on the doormat.'

Unless she'd been what? wondered Jenny. Nigel had checked himself. She knew Nicola well enough to guess at various experiments with pills and conceivably needles.

Presently Nigel telephoned again. 'No reply.'

Jenny brought them Remy Martin.

Nigel's boss, now openly lecherous, got up unsteadily and said he was going to a strip-club. 'Coming, Nigel?'

'No, thank you. It's very kind but I don't think I will.'

'Please yourself.'

'I'm a bit worried, actually.'

Jenny thought he was right to be worried: but agreed with him that there was nothing he could do.

At last the restaurant grew quiet and nearly empty. The bar was closed and Jenny had finished her steamy evening's work.

She went and sat with Nigel and smoked one of his Disque Bleu cigarettes.

'What do you think,' she said, 'about bashing down the door of her flat?'

'Oh, Jenny, for God's sake —' Jenny recognised Nigel's tone. She was always getting it from people when she made helpful and constructive suggestions.

Before Nigel could elaborate, as he was plainly about to do, there was a rattling descent of the wooden stairs. A tall, fair-haired girl stumbled forward into the light.

'Tamara!' shouted Nigel. 'Where have you been? Where's Nicola? What *happened?*'

'I don't know.'

'Sit down,' said Jenny.

Tamara sat down. She refused brandy but accepted coffee with relief. She was not making sense.

Nigel yammered at her but Jenny told him to be quiet. They waited while Tamara recovered her breath and her equilibrium.

While they waited Jenny thought sourly of her plea to the world at lunchtime: stay out of trouble, please please stay out of trouble, until we've all had a rest.

'Lots of men,' Tamara finally said. 'Lots of men in a room. They made us take all our clothes off. They were horrible. They let me go. But they kept Nicola. They said . . . '

'*What?*'

'They were sitting looking at her, and she was standing there with nothing on, nothing at all . . . They looked at her and they said she was the sort to . . . '

'*To what?*'

'Make them all enough to retire on.'

2

'Let's go there,' shouted Nigel, 'let's get the police and go there!'

'Hush,' said Jenny. She caught her full pink lower lip under her little white teeth and her eyes rolled upwards to the inky ceiling. She was thinking. There were several courses of action possible. Several directions in which to turn, several people who could instantly be telephoned. Unfortunately these courses were all useless. Without more knowledge everything was useless. The vital thing now was to see what this was all about.

'Why aren't we going there?' shouted Nigel again.

'Presently, pet. No hurry.'

'*But she may be—*'

'Think,' said Jenny, who was thinking aloud to herself. 'If they let Tamara go they must have been off themselves. Wherever she is, it's not where she was. They've popped her into a nice, safe hidey-hole. Must have. What we need now is a bit of history. Tell, Tamara.'

Tamara's clothes had the untidy look of someone who had dressed in the dark or too quickly. There was a smear of dirt across her cheek. She had lost one glove but she still held her bag.

The last customer had left the restaurant. No one took any notice of Tamara. The manager was in a far corner counting money. All the unfulfilled waitresses had gone except one, who was morosely putting chairs on to tables.

Jenny, Tamara and Nigel sat in a single pool of light in a large, empty area of darkness. Tamara accepted a cigarette from Jenny and a light from Nigel and tried to tell them what happened.

The taxi had started. They thought the driver was going forward to pick up Nigel and Dave Maddox, and were surprised when it suddenly turned into a side-street.

'We shouted at him,' said Tamara. 'He just went faster.'

'Stop,' said Jenny. 'Wait. This taxi. Where and how did you get it?'

'Actually there was something odd about that,' said Nigel.

'Tell.'

'We came out of a pub. A taxi appeared. Providentially, out of the blue. Swam up out of the fog.'

'Waiting for you.'

'A chap hailed it. A chap who'd been in the pub and left ten minutes before.'

'Waiting for you. Waiting to identify you to the taxi-driver.'

'The chap talked to the driver, then just walked off. The driver told us the chap wanted to be taken to Highgate and the driver wouldn't do it in the fog.'

'Describe chap.'

'Seedy little man, woolly muffler, flapping umbrella. Respectable as hell.'

'Describe driver.'

'Muffled up to the eyebrows.'

'First chap, seedy one. He saw you in the pub?'

'Yes, stared at the girls. Well, damn it, every man in the bar stared at the girls.'

Jenny nodded. Tamara was a Nordic beauty, an obvious model, an eyeful. Nicola, in her dark and strange and very special style, was perhaps even more spectacular, more obviously sexy, more excitingly neurotic.

'He had a good look at the girls, he heard you talking, he heard where you were going to have dinner. Did he go off and telephone?'

'No. I don't know. How do I know? Of course, he could have.'

'He absolutely must have, pet. So – bogus taxi summoned. Lurks near pub, flag down, not for hire. You come out, you're identified, taxi picks you up, knows where you're going before you tell him. So – you pass fake breakdown. Out you get and push, birds stay in taxi. Taxi off. Then what, Tamara?'

They had not dared jump out of the taxi which was driven fast and jumped two red lights.

It finally turned into a small dark street, turned again into a mews, and then gone right into a big garage. Another car was already in the garage, the little grey two-seater.

The garage door had shut with a clang and it had been very dark. Nicola had begun to scream and Tamara thought she had screamed too.

'Then they opened the door and pulled me out.'

'Who's they?'

'I don't know. It was dark. I don't know. I tried to fight but they were too strong.'

She had been hustled through a door and up some stone stairs and into a big bright room. Nicola came up after her, between two men, struggling.

'What did the men look like?'

'Just like . . . men. I don't know.'

'Big? Small? Rough? Smooth?'

'Yes. I don't know. One of them was the man in the car. With the red moustache.'

Two other men, frightening men, were waiting for them in the bright room. These men told them to undress.

'Why were they frightening?'

'One was big,' said Tamara after a pause. She began to shudder uncontrollably. Jenny again offered her brandy but she said she wanted coffee.

'This big man,' said Jenny, bringing the coffee, 'was he dark or fair?'

'Dark. Rather dark.'

'Anything else?'

'He was . . . ' She frowned. 'You know. Just a biggish man, rather dark.'

She remembered the cold in the room. There was ice inside the windows. The breath of all of them steamed in the room under the single, bright naked bulb. Tamara had not wanted to undress, but she and Nicola had been made to strip.

'And the other man?' said Jenny, forcing herself to be gentle and patient with this intolerably unhelpful girl. 'The other frightening man?'

'He . . . had a small head. A very small head. He was American.'

'Tall? Thin? Fat?'

'Quite thin. Just . . . ordinary. Except for his head.'

'Was the room furnished?'

'Furnished?' Tamara looked vague.

'Chairs?' said Jenny soothingly. 'Tables? Carpets?'

'Oh, I see. No. Just some boxes. They sat on boxes.'

They had looked at the girls, standing naked in the bitterly cold room. One of the men had whistled. This had annoyed the man with the very small head.

Then they had started inspecting Tamara.

'Inspecting?'

'Sort of like the doctor.'

One of them had listened to her chest with a stethoscope. They had looked at her teeth. The end of the stethoscope had been very cold.

They had made her speak – read some lines from a book.

'What book?'

'I don't know. A story.'

'Go on.'

They had carefully inspected her forearms and upper arms.

Finally she had been measured.

The man with the small head said: 'No.'

'He said,' Tamara explained, 'that I was too long to ship home. And he only needed one now. Another soon, but only one now.'

The dark man protested, but the man with the small head was

in charge and the others did what he said. The big dark man was more frightening, but the man with the small head was the one who was in charge.

Tamara was allowed to dress. She was shivering and frightened, and her fingers were numb with cold. She dressed as quickly as she could.

She was taken into another room, tiny, almost a cupboard. It was cold and pitch-dark except for a crack of light under the door. The door was locked. She waited there a long time. She could hear voices and bumps but nothing she could understand.

Then the door opened. Nicola was dressing. She looked terrified. The man with the small head said: 'This one's our pension, boys. She'll make enough for us all to retire.'

One of the men came for Tamara and took her out by another door and down different stairs and out into a different street. She did not know the name of this street. There was no one about – no cars, no policemen, nothing. There seemed to be only warehouses, and terraces of empty and crumbling villas. There were no doorbells to ring. She ran. She found herself presently in the Fulham Road, and had known her way to The Joint, and had run there, thinking they would protect and comfort her.

'Nicola,' said Nigel harshly.

'Yes,' said Jenny. 'We ought to peer. Useless I'm sure, but silly not to.' She turned to Tamara and said gently: 'If we come with you, and we go in my car, can you find this place again?'

'Yes,' said Tamara.

'Come on, then.'

'No,' cried Tamara, 'I can't, it's cold, I'm frightened.'

'Police,' said Nigel.

'Later,' said Jenny.

Jenny pulled on trousers and suede boots and two more sweaters over her sweater. They went to her Mini.

'Damn, frosted up.'

Jenny squeezed de-icer from an aerosol and told Nigel to rub.

She started the car.

'Get in the back, Nigel. Tamara, will you sit in the front, love? Then you can show me where to go.'

Tamara was trembling and reluctant. But she obeyed. She folded her tall and elegant body into the front seat. Jenny was relieved. She was asking a lot of the girl.

'Why are we going?' wailed Tamara.

'Oh, it seems wise. We might learn something. And then, I mean, it's cold, suppose their car didn't start or the garage door stuck?'

'Jenny,' said Nigel sharply, 'what if they are there? What can we do?'

'We might think of something. Is this it, Tamara?'

'N—no, I don't think so. Further on.'

It was still foggy and still bitterly cold. At each corner Jenny stopped and Tamara pondered.

Jenny's hands were cold on the wheel. She could hear Nigel breathing hard in the back, and she felt sorry for him, because she knew Nicola. For this reason she was more gentle and patient with Tamara than many of her friends would have believed possible.

After ten minutes and many corners it became obvious that they had overshot.

'It's this fog,' said Tamara fretfully. 'How can I see?'

'Try,' said Jenny.

They turned and crawled east again.

'That's it!'

Jenny stopped the car. 'Sure?'

'Yes, yes! I remember the poster. It's a picture of me.'

It was: Tamara in a yellow shirt, popping a sweet into a wide, wide mouth.

Jenny turned sharp right and drove slowly down a dark narrow street.

The fog seemed denser. The little engine burbled loudly between dark icy walls.

'I don't like this,' said Nigel.

'Not where I'd choose to live myself,' murmured Jenny.

'I mean I'm scared.'

'Yes, love, very prudent of you, who isn't?'

A darker black yawned to the left between the black of the buildings.

'Here,' said Tamara.

'Is it a cul-de-sac?'

'A what?'

'Can we drive out of the other end?' asked Jenny patiently.

'No. The garage is the other end.'

'Then I think,' said Jenny, 'it might be foolish to drive in.'

She turned the Mini, stopped the engine and switched out the lights.

'You stay here, Tamara. Keep warm. Come on, Nigel.'

'I'm not staying here alone!' wailed Tamara.

She insisted on coming with them, saying that it was frightening but less frightening than sitting alone in the dark so near the big dark man's big bright room.

They walked softly into the pitch-black yard. There was no light from the building at the end, or from the faceless bulk of the buildings on either side.

No torch, thought Jenny. Stupid.

They nearly cannoned into the big metal door of the garage. It felt cold and rough and gritty, as though patches of rust had been painted over.

Nothing could be seen. Nothing could be heard. No chink of light showed from anywhere. The ice-cold mist seemed to invade their mouths and noses and grope downwards and chill the deep warm vulnerable places inside them.

Tamara moaned.

'Shh,' said Jenny.

They watched and listened. No sound, no light.

'They've gone,' said Nigel harshly. He was very close to Jenny but invisible in the blackness. *'Where have they taken her?*

30

Why?'

'Hard to say, love. What about this door, now that we're here?'

They groped for a handle, finding each others' numbed hands, and, at last, near the ground, a wide metal handle.

'Roll-over type. Bound to be locked.'

It was not locked.

'Lift quietly.'

It was impossible to lift quietly. Possibly the fog blanketed the noise, but it seemed shocking – a great, grinding, unlubricated scream of metal, although the door lifted quite easily and smoothly.

They groped forward, and Jenny barked her shin on shin-high metal. It was the rear bumper of a car.

'The one you pushed, I bet.'

Nigel lit his lighter and they immediately recognised the little grey two-seater.

'How vexing,' said Jenny. 'They wouldn't have left it here unless they'd stolen it. So it can't be traced to them.'

'But it can! They left it here!'

'No, love, if you think for a second. This sweet place can't be traced to them either. They just borrowed it.'

'They'll never come back, then.'

'Well, it wouldn't be sensible, would it? Let's try the door to the inside.'

They found the door Tamara had been hustled through. It was locked. There was no other door. There was no noise or light anywhere.

'So much for that,' said Jenny. 'Let's go and talk to some bluebottles.'

'I suppose,' said Nigel, 'they wouldn't have left something in the back of the car?'

'We might as well look.'

Nigel groped round to the driver's door and found the handle. It seemed to be locked. He swore softly. But it was not locked, only old and stiff. The door opened with a squeak. The interior of the car smelt of petrol and rubber and scent.

'Joy,' said Jenny, sniffing.

'I gave it to her,' said Nigel thickly.

'Poor sweet.'

The scent evoked her for them both. Jenny could sense that Nigel was almost screaming with longing and worry and fear.

He lit his lighter again.

It was an untidy little car, with split upholstery, and sweet-papers spilling out of the ashtray, and cracks in the glass of the instrument dials. It smelt of petrol and rubber and the Joy which evoked Nicola and of cigarettes and dust.

There was nothing on the seat or the floor or in the pigeon-hole or the pockets in the doors.

'What's that at the back?' said Tamara.

She pointed at something on the narrow shelf behind the seat.

'A glove.'

'Or a bedroom slipper?'

Nigel reached for it. He had an impression, through numbed fingertips, of something torpedo-shaped and made of stiff fur.

'Yes, a slipper.'

'A slipper. In the back of a car. You know, I have a feeling that someone's got over-excited and made a very silly mistake. I do believe,' murmured Jenny, 'that one really only ever wins anything because someone else makes a bloomer.'

'How the hell,' said Nigel shrilly, 'could a slipper be important?'

Jenny knew why he sounded shrill, and she thought he had a right to. 'I don't know,' she said. 'Let's take it along, anyway.'

Nigel's lighter blew out as he shut the car door (an appalling clang). In a darkness blacker than before because of the light they groped back into the yard.

'Shut the garage door?'

'Oh yes,' said Jenny. 'Let's be tidy.'

At this moment a car could be heard turning off the main road and coming down the side road towards the yard. The glow of its headlights was now dimly visible through the fog in the mouth of the yard. The engine grew louder and the light brighter.

'I don't hugely care for this,' murmured Jenny. 'Let's trot away.'

She led the way, running quietly, towards the black flank of the building to the left and then along the wall towards the opening into the street. Tamara's smart boots were leather-soled and her running was loudly percussive.

Then the car turned into the yard and stopped. A spotlight came on between the fog-lamps. It cut through the thick air and lit the little grey car in the open garage.

Jenny stopped and gestured. The three froze, flat against the empty wall of the building.

The new car was invisible in the fog behind the glare of its lights. It seemed to be a big car; the idling motor sounded big and powerful.

A door opened. A man with gingery whiskers ran to the garage and opened the door of the two-seater. After a moment he ran out again and stood in the glare of the spotlight. He gestured, palms down: 'No.'

As he ran back towards the big car its engine revved.

Jenny realised, with a sick sense of folly, that the car was going to turn. This was not a night for backing out of narrow gateways. Its rear would swing towards them, so that its lights raked the wall opposite: or else its rear would swing away, so that they would be caught, like butterflies on pins, in the powerful headlamps.

Their friends would not like finding visitors.

'Which way?' Jenny muttered.

The back of the car swung away. The spotlight swept along the black shiny wall towards them.

'Oh, God,' said Nigel, 'I'm frightened.'

'So am I,' said Jenny. 'Run like hell.'

3

They ran like hell towards the entrance of the yard. The big car shifted into forward gear and the spotlight swung towards the entrance. Jenny, Tamara and Nigel reached the entrance just as the spotlight did. The car was twenty yards from them. They were vividly lit. The car's motor roared and it leapt forward. Tamara slipped and screamed. Nigel grabbed her arm as she fell and dragged her across the gaping emptiness of the entrance. The car rocketed towards them, the noise and glare intensifying with tremendous speed. They stumbled clear of the entrance and the car missed Tamara by inches. There was a screech of tyres and the car swerved and rocked and it stopped, slewed sideways, just short of the far side of the little dark street. By the time the driver had backed clear Nigel was in the back seat of Jenny's Mini and Tamara (moaning) and Jenny were in the front.

Jenny failed to start the engine first time. Tamara screamed again. Jenny wanted to scream too. The engine fired and Jenny accelerated away up the street as the big car behind them accelerated too.

'Lights!' shouted Nigel.

'No, love,' said Jenny.

She swerved left-handed into the main road, the wheels screaming and the little car rocking violently but holding the road. Jenny murmured a prayer of thanks for the Mini's front-wheel drive and nippiness and road-holding.

But it was not terribly fast. The weight of three people slowed it down, enfeebled the acceleration of the tiny engine. A long straight and the big car must catch them. Now, after a short straight, its headlights blazed in Jenny's driving-mirror. It was only feet behind them.

'You're mad!' shouted Nigel. 'You're mad!'

Jenny cornered savagely again, into another little dark street. This took Nigel by surprise and he was hurled across the cramped back seat. The big car screeched round the corner behind them.

Jenny turned again. She was the sort of woman driver who terrifies male passengers, not because she was bad (she thought) but because she was extremely good. Now she was terrified herself.

Each time she turned she gained a few yards on the big heavy car; in every straight it roared up behind them. Once it touched – a clang which nearly upset the Mini at fifty-five miles an hour. Jenny swerved right and they gained a few yards and the big car hurtled close to them again.

Tamara screamed without stopping.

Who would ever have dreamt, thought Jenny, that they'd come back again?

The slipper, she thought. They came back for the slipper.

They turned, turned, turned, doubled back, jigged through little mews and across empty main roads.

Jenny wondered about guns behind them. Presumably not, or they would have used them by now. Why not?

They shot red lights, nearly killed a solitary bicyclist and were nearly killed by a rumbling vegetable lorry. The big car thundered after them, lights glaring in the fog, screaming and rolling on the corners, gaining with every yard of straight.

They're trying to kill us, thought Jenny. Why? Why is borrowing a slipper grounds for murder?

Tamara screamed and screamed.

Jenny had no plan except to go round corners as often and as fast as possible. Suddenly she had a plan. She remembered a place where she had been taken to tea as a child. Tea with an ambassador. Tea with foreign cakes.

West of Kensington Gardens Jenny got fifty yards clear of the big car. She slowed and turned towards the little dark opening she remembered.

'It's close,' she murmured, 'but I think, I think . . . '

There were big metal bollards across the cobbles of the side road. These had been put up long ago to keep out the carts of the vulgar; they still made the small, quiet street into a footpath. The Mini nosed between them. Each side scraped.

'Oh dear,' said Jenny.

The car stuck. She accelerated hard. There was a grinding metallic noise and the Mini shuddered and screeched and went through and Jenny drove away fast.

'No door handles,' she murmured. 'Will we ever get out?'

The big car skidded and turned and hurled itself towards the side-street. The driver didn't know about the bollards and didn't see them in time. The car hit a bollard with a clang like the end of the world and climbed up it and the bonnet was a mess.

Jenny slowed down. 'Nigel, can you see if they're all dead?'

Nigel craned to see out of the steamy rear window. 'One isn't,' he reported.

Jenny looked round. The man with ginger whiskers had scrambled out of the wreckage and was limping after them.

'What a *bore,*' said Jenny. It was possible this man had a gun or throwing-knife. It was possible one or more of his friends would crawl out of the big car and join him. It was tempting to try and get him, and take him to Sandro for questioning: tempting but unwise.

Jenny tried to remember the other end of the street, and had a sudden sick feeling of dismay.

'We may have a problem now,' she said cheerfully.

The problem was a huge wooden beam across the mouth of the side-street, hinged, open by day to admit tradesmen, bolted down at night. It was quite high.

The Mini jolted down two shallow steps, then drove up to the beam and tried to nose underneath. The beam touched the roof of the car just above the windscreen. Jenny put her foot down. There was another grinding noise and some glass broke. Then the car squeezed under and through.

'My poor little car. Lucky the tyres weren't too full. Have you still got that slipper?'

'I think I dropped it when they tried to run us over,' said Nigel, who had forgotten about the slipper.

'Gracious, all their trouble for nothing,' said Jenny. 'I wonder why the slipper's so important. Meanwhile I suppose we'd better tell someone about all this.'

Some disapproving policemen looked at the ruins of the big car. It was deserted. Any corpses had been taken away.

The car had been stolen at 4 p.m. from an angry doctor in Mill Hill.

The rooms above the garage were deserted too. Tamara whimpered when she saw them again.

Jenny pictured the scene, memory of which made Tamara whimper. Two girls, one tall and fair, one a little shorter with deep breasts and long black hair, standing side by side like slaves at auction, like meat in a market, being coldly inspected.

A nasty scene.

Gooseflesh on the girls' thighs and bellies. Their breasts white and pathetic in the harsh glare of the naked bulb. Their faces terrified and uncomprehending.

Jenny felt angry. This was a beastly way to treat people.

The police said the premises were empty and to let; they had been unoccupied for two months. Eventual demolition was expected. The wooden boxes were empty.

They also knew by now that the grey two-seater had been stolen some days before. Its owner was the recently married son of a Balham greengrocer. He had paid £130 for the car and was surprised that anyone should bother to nick it.

Nigel looked sick. Jenny guessed that he was also imagining the scene in the bright bare room.

The fur slipper had disappeared from the entrance into the yard. A detective remarked that if you dropped yesterday's newspaper in this part of London someone would pick it up and find a use for it.

'You should have come to us straight away, sir,' said a Station Officer sadly to Nigel.

'Well, you see,' said Jenny cozeningly, 'we thought there was just a chance our chum might still be there if we rushed.'

'What *could* you have done, Miss?'

'We might have thought of something.'

Nigel described Nicola. Five foot four, superb figure. No, not one of your skinny model types. No, *not* plump.

Long dark hair. Very pale face. Eyes dark blue. Usually wore false eyelashes. Usual scent Joy. Clothes when last seen a red mini-skirt, black thigh-boots, red and black shirt of heavy silk, black leather coat with heavy brass buttons. No distinguishing marks.

When he tried to describe her face the shorthand writer thought he was exaggerating.

He was not exaggerating.

Nicola lay on her back on a bed in a dusty basement room. Her mouth was slightly open and her eyes were shut. Her face was paler even than usual – drained of blood, of life. It was so white that it was grey.

It would have been easy to imagine her dead, except for the very slight and slow movement of her breast under the grubby blanket.

A man stood looking down at her. A sad respectable man in a woolly muffler.

He turned, switched off the dangling overhead light, went out of the room and shut the door. He locked the door.

When the police had exhausted their questions, Jenny tried a few. But there were no answers.

The police offered no theory about Nicola's kidnapping. They knew of no recent case even remotely similar.

No bells of recognition were rung by the description (Tamara's almost useless description) of the American with the very small head. Nobody had heard of an American with a very small head.

And London was full of big dark men, many of them frightening. Gingery whiskers abounded, on the faces of the just and of the unjust. And sad respectable little men with woolly mufflers and flapping umbrellas could be seen in their hundreds queueing outside cinemas where nude films were shown.

At last, late at night, they were all taken home in police cars.

'You should have come to us straight away, Miss. What you did was dangerous and irresponsible.'

'I *know*, I *weep*. Good night, Officer.'

'Why the hell didn't you go to the police straight away?' asked Sandro. He seemed quite angry.

Jenny was lying almost horizontally in a deep armchair rendered deeper by the collapse of its springs. 'Don't *rail* at me, love. The good blue gentlemen would have clumped up demanding entry, and no useful purpose would have been served.'

'No useful purpose was served. And you damned nearly got yourself killed, you and your stupid little friends. Suppose they'd had even one gun?'

Jenny shuddered. 'The very thought makes me thirsty. Be a love and get me another whisky and soda.'

'You drink too much.'

Sandro nevertheless got up from the sofa where he was lying

and prowled over to the cupboard where Jenny kept her drinks.

'Get me one too, will you, chum?' said Colly, apparently waking up.

Sandro grunted. As he squirted soda into two glasses he looked as though he might at any moment explode into violent physical activity or into a passion of rage, or burst out singing, or seduce someone.

Colly looked incapable of raising a full glass to his lips.

They were in Jenny's flat, which was the top floor of a rickety office building near Covent Garden market. The fruit lorries made a nightmare noise early in the morning, but it was large and bright and could be made warm. It was very feminine and untidy and quite often full of people who were surprised to find each other at the same party.

'By the way,' said Jenny, 'are either of you staying here?'

'Not me,' said Colly.

'Good God, no indeed! Excitement I can bear, but discomfort and squalor are insupportable.'

'This flat is not squalid.'

It was not altogether squalid. The furniture was ill-matched and shabby, but gay-coloured and clean. The pictures on the walls, many hanging quite straight, were a charming, higgledy-piggledy mixture of things Jenny liked: Some had cost her shillings or even pence; one, a Raeburn with a hilly landscape behind a solemn elderly man, was worth several thousand pounds.

Opening off the sitting-room was a passage and Jenny's bedroom, another bedroom, a bathroom, and a big kitchen, and there was a door opening onto the steep wooden stairs which led down behind the floors of offices to the street. The street was often covered with the bruised and oozing remnants of fruit and vegetables – with cabbage leaves and brussels sprouts, with burst plums and the awful ruins of tomatoes. Upstairs in Jenny's flat none of these things were permitted. Her own bedroom was large and soft and frilly and brightly coloured, and

THE MAN WITH THE TINY HEAD

full of old teddy bears, and photographs of ponies and puppies, and stockings and underwear. A tiara hung negligently on the corner of a looking-glass; on the other corner hung a lot of dog-leads. On the bed lay six King Charles spaniels in a heap. It was the bedroom of a girl who had had a happy childhood.

'You both have such boring rich ideas,' said Jenny. 'One frayed curtain and you assume a place is full of cockroaches. Where are you staying?'

'With Flavia, where else?' said Sandro.

'Where is Flavia?' asked Colly.

'She has taken very nearly the whole of—which square?'

'Well, which square?'

'The square Flavia has taken very nearly the whole of. For several months. Eaton Square.'

'Are you two matey together?' asked Jenny.

'We *adore* each other.'

'Is Flavia making a film?'

'The largest in history. She is to be queen – which queen is she to be?'

'Well, which queen?'

'Some queen. Absurd miscasting, as I tell her. She will always be an American bourgeoisie. You must know about her film. Even you, Jenny, can hardly have evaded the oceans of sickening publicity.'

'I can hardly read, you know. I hardly ever went to any sort of school.'

'Shocking. I really deplore the English upper classes.'

'You love the English upper classes. There's no snob like a Wop snob.'

Sandro laughed.

'So neither of you are staying. Beasts. Just as well, really. I've had enough excitement for one night.'

'Abduction, attempted murder, so tiring.'

'Yes, I'm bushed. And so, so thirsty, beautiful Sandro . . .

'Get your own drink.'

'Colly, Angel . . . ?'

'Don't look at me, darling. Pleasant though I know you find it. I couldn't move to save your life. That telephone this morning really took it out of me. I'd forgotten telephones could get so goddam *heavy*.'

'So what,' said Jenny from the sideboard, 'do we make of this evening's fun and games?'

'What I find strange,' said Sandro, 'is their fussiness. They catch two plump young trout and they throw one back.'

'We know they only needed one.'

'Who only needs one? How is it possible only to need one? One for what?'

'She's gonna make all their fortunes,' said Colly, 'and she's standing there naked when they say so. I don't think we have any doubts what her job's gonna be.'

'Sure, *caro*, but why only one and why that one?'

'They checked her health,' said Jenny, 'they checked her accent, they checked her arms for hypodermic jabs.'

'Is she on the hard stuff?'

'Oh no. Not a girl-friend of Nigel's. I mean, I shouldn't think so. He's so *earnestly* respectable. Tamara certainly not. In spite of being such a dish she's really rather a po-faced girl.'

'Po-faced? What is this new misuse of your language?'

'There's no one so pompous, is there, as a pompous Wop . . . . A large, well-organised, unarmed murderous gang who kept a clever nutty girl and tossed a dull one back into the water. Loopy behaviour.'

'Loopy? Please attempt to address me in English.'

Jenny laughed and they all lay back (except that Colly had not moved) and thought quite hard about the implications of the kidnapping.

'They were all ready, weren't they? Ready to leap into instant action.'

'At the command of an American. Who talked of shipping her home.'

'He came over to get one, perhaps.'

'Customs, immigration,' said Sandro. 'Someone ought to remember a man with a tiny head.'

'Customs, immigration,' said Jenny. 'Someone may see Nicola.'

'I think not,' said Sandro.

'America's full of girls,' said Colly with evident effort. 'Every goddam state in the Union is lousy with girls who peel off and tie themselves in knots for a few bucks. If all this American needs is a naked lady, why go to all the trouble and expense?'

'He wants English girls,' said Jenny. 'And he's fussy about accent.'

'Would their accents be different, those two?' said Sandro.

'Oh yes,' said Jenny. 'A little, but a lot, if you know what I mean.'

'Doesn't mean a goddam thing to me,' said Colly.

'But we must accept that it is important to them,' said Sandro. 'So is that slipper. Why did they try to kill you because you had one slipper?'

'Didn't want to break the pair,' said Colly. 'Nobody wants to lose just the one. I speak as a man with a dozen left gloves.'

'What a terrible pity,' said Sandro, 'your Nigel did not hold on to it. It would lead us to them, I think.'

'How? Why?'

'I suppose we must find out.'

'The beautiful blonde,' said Colly, 'is eliminated from the Miss Imported Call Girl contest because she speaks a little common. Or because she is not full of pin-holes. Or because she is full of pin-holes. Or because she is too tall. This guy is goddam hard to please.'

'We will not easily find any of these men,' said Sandro. 'We cannot argue from the men to the racket. Therefore we must argue from the racket to the men.'

'I wish I knew what any of that meant,' said Jenny.

'I have to go home, do I?' said Colly faintly, 'and hunt all over the United States for a small-headed guy running a one-girl brothel? Who, on his way to the bathroom in the middle of the night, has only one slipper?'

'You know this Nicola,' said Sandro to Jenny.

'Yes. Not well.'

'Describe her exactly.'

Jenny described her physically, then in terms of character and habits. 'Fast-moving girl,' she said. 'Apt to be where the action is. Noticeable. Rather a—a desperate hunt for fun, I think. Drinks quite a lot, smokes too much. Gambles a bit, a late-night girl.'

'She does not sound clever.'

'She is clever. Clever, neurotic, a bit of an emotional mess I should think. That's why Nigel was good for her. He's dull but he's intelligent and square. Sane. Normal.'

'He may be useful. This girl. She is smart?'

'Clothes? Oh yes. Spends a lot of money.'

'I mean socially. She is *ben nata?*'

'Oh, snobwise, yes, very much so. A bit above Nigel's station really. What worries me is that this sort of thing, whatever it is she's in for, may tumble her right over the edge.'

The light in the basement room was switched on again.

The man with the woolly muffler tiptoed to the bed. Nicola lay white and lifeless. The man pulled back the blanket. Nicola was in bra and pants only. She was beautiful. The man sat down on the bed beside her. He began pinching and caressing and exploring her flaccid body. His hands were obscene and he did obscene things with them. He was dribbling slightly and the breath whistled through the hairs of his nose.

Footsteps, loud and commanding footsteps, approached along the passage outside.

The man in the woolly muffler stood up and whipped the blanket back over Nicola and smoothed it and turned to face the big dark man who came in.

'In final essence,' said Sandro, 'this girl is worth finding?'

'Oh yes,' said Jenny. 'Poor little Nigel, of course we must find her. Besides, they'll want more. I mean, this is horrid, it ought to be stopped. And maybe he's already got several. I wonder how many juicy girls have disappeared recently.'

'The police say none.'

'They say none they know of. None quite like that.'

Sandro shrugged. 'Girls disappear all the time. It is part of the British way of life. They disappear to be tarts, to take off their clothes in nightclubs, to drinks baths—'

'Baths, pet? To drink *baths!*'

'I mean meths. The country crawls with girls who have disappeared.'

'The question is whether America does too. Oh dear, how difficult.'

'Too difficult for this time of night,' said Colly. 'I'm gonna creep to bed.'

'I also,' said Sandro.

'With Flavia?'

'Probably not.' Sandro sighed. 'A film star with bourgeois morals. I detest everything about all Anglo-Saxons.'

He put on his fur-lined coat, which was less rigorously English than his other clothes. He and Jenny kissed lightly.

'Good night, fatty.'

'Good night, *carina*. If they got your car number you will be murdered within forty-eight hours.'

'Why?'

'Because of the slipper.'

'Yes, it's rather a worry. Love to Flavia.'

Colly had struggled to his feet. His short, mousy hair stood on end and he yawned cavernously. He also kissed Jenny, but he groaned as he did so.

'Good night, Tarzan,' said Jenny.

Colly waved as though his hand were heavy. He and Sandro

disappeared down the wooden stairs.

Jenny felt suddenly too tired to move. She sank back among the collapsed springs of the armchair. She brooded about the evening, trying to make sense of it. Then she fell asleep. Presently she shifted in her sleep and a spring twanged and woke her. She shivered and stretched and got up and went into her bedroom. She threw off her clothes, sending them into various corners of the room. She got into bed without much disturbing all the King Charles spaniels who were asleep on top of it. Their weight and warmth was comforting. She fell asleep instantly.

Early next morning a man in a woolly muffler, and with a flapping umbrella, and with a look of sad respectability, went to County Hall and looked up the registered owner of a car whose number he had.

4

At the moment that the man in the woolly muffler emerged, hurrying, from County Hall, Nigel Heywood arrived at his office. He was late. He was feeling sick and old. He had a headache. His sleep had been punctuated by shuddering thoughts of Nicola.

He had a brief meeting with his boss, whose eyeballs were yellower than usual.

'Ever find those girls?'

'One.'

'Yours?'

'Yours.'

'Damn. I might have stuck around. I got hold of a very ropey old do at the Candlelight. What's become of Nicola, then?'

'We don't know,' said Nigel.

Back in his own small office, among proofs of advertisements and modish pin-ups, Nigel sank his head on to his arms.

Nicola.

At the moment that Nigel groaned as he thought of Nicola, Sandro drank his fifteenth very small cup of very strong black coffee. He was sitting in the big upstairs drawing room of the copious premises taken by his ex-wife (and paid for by Galactic Studios, Los Angeles). The room was furnished and decorated with a strict regard to uniformity of style; it seemed less a room than an exhibition of unadventurous design.

'*Che caffe cattivo,*' said Sandro, frowning at a gilt wall-bracket. Sandro was dressed as though for a strapping tramp in Wiltshire, in a heavy ribbed sweater and cavalry twill trousers.

'If you don't like it, darling, why drink it?' said Flavia, who was writing postcards at an imitation Empire desk.

'To stay awake,' said Sandro.

'Itchy-coo, poor ickle fing, was it tired then? You've been up outa bed for a whole hour.'

'How you are strenuous! I can see I shall have no peace until you begin filming.'

'You know what you are? You're a bum.'

'What should I do? Dig a ditch? Drive a taxi?'

'Work, Goddammit.'

'*Perche?* What possible point?'

'Oh, Sandro,' sighed Flavia May, 'how I would have loved you if you were a man.'

Flavia was romantically swathed in miles of violet silk; she called the garment, with her usual directness, a dressing-gown: but the effect belonged at a court ball in a period of ostentatious expenditure. From the top of this pyramid of purple emerged a bright gold head and a large, soft, sexy face with shrewd blue eyes.

Sandro looked at her with affection and impatience. 'Storekeeper's daughter,' he said.

'That's me. The hell with all flabby aristocrats.'

'Pennsylvania Dutch. You know something? I'm surprised your religion allows you to *go* to the movies.'

Flavia looked at him with affection and impatience. 'When you were my husband—'

'I am your husband.'

'Jack is my husband.'

'Jack is a very nice guy, and if you must have a paramour—'

Flavia shrugged, causing a liquefication through the copious billows of silk. She turned back to her postcard.

Shooting starts Tuesday, she wrote. *Great to be back at work. London weather stinks. Kisses, F.* She addressed it to the elderly head of a famous medical school in Michigan. The picture on the front was of a kitten in a pink-lined basket.

'Lazing away on that yacht,' said Flavia. 'Who ever heard of yachting in the Mediterranean at this time of year?'

'It was something to do,' said Sandro apologetically.

'Bum. Bum in spades. It really is a shame.'

Sandro thought briefly, and with no pleasure, of the sharp recent sea-battle between his motor-yacht and the heroin-laden fishing-boat of the Ornello brothers. His bazookas had been decisive; his mate had machine-gunned the gangsters in the water until Sandro stopped him. Two of his own crew had been killed (sturdy Ponzesi, brave men and born to the sea) one of whom was the mate's son.

Flavia selected a postcard for the daughter of a drugstore owner in Scranton who had married (beneath him) her cousin. The picture was the Paolo Ucelli boar-hunt in the National Gallery.

'So what will you do these next few weeks?'

'I shall go possibly to the races at Newbury. There is some furniture I want to see at Wilton. I foresee an exhausting time.'

He wondered whether Jenny ought to disappear, and whether she could disappear totally enough, and why one girl had been kidnapped and kept and one kidnapped and released.

He wanted to take Flavia immediately to bed, but he knew this was not possible.

Very likely, in the dark, they would not have seen Jenny's number-plate. Her lights were off. It was foggy. Knowing Jenny her car would have been filthy and the number-plates, at this muddy time of year, filthiest of all.

Very likely Jenny was safe. Relatively. For a while.

At the moment that Sandro started on his sixteenth cup of black coffee, Jenny was counting her wages on a table at The Joint.

'What I think, love,' she said, 'is that you owe me another eleven and six.'

'God of battles,' shouted the manager. 'I've worked this out with the utmost care. Eleven and six? Eleven and six? Eleven and six? Where do you get eleven and six?'

'By adding up,' said Jenny, 'on my fingers.'

'We can afford eleven and six,' said the manager with dignity. 'I admit nothing. This is an *ex gratia* payment to avoid *nastiness.*'

It was nearly lunchtime. Jenny had consented to dispense wine for the lunch rush and the dinner rush, and to finish after dinner. Consequently she was in her working clothes, in which (or the absence of which) the manager was not interested, his own preoccupations running in different directions. Jenny had become fond of him, and he of Jenny. Their rows had been frequent but minor.

'I'm sorry you're going,' he said, putting eleven and six on top of the small pile of money on the table where they were drinking Chambery together.

'Thank you, love. I'm quite weepy too, but my feet get so fearfully itchy.'

'What will you do now?'

'If I could *but* answer. Nothing so cosy, I'm sure.'

The restaurant was like all night-time places in day-time (although it was allegedly a day-time place also) – unkempt and grubby. Jenny found it depressing, and was depressed also by the thought that all three of them, the previous night, had seen the slipper.

Tamara's face was presumably traceable, though she was by no means a top model and her cool, smooth features were not distinctive. Could they have seen Nigel properly? Surely not. In any case they couldn't all three hide forever.

At the moment that Jenny picked up her crinkling and jingling wages, Colly Tucker surfaced, with a succession of groans, in his room at the Connaught. To the waiter who brought him his coffee he said something about a late session at the Clermont.

He had accepted, with bitter reluctance, a job for the morning. With his third cigarette he sat up in bed and did it: he rang up the police.

He dropped a few important names. Presently he was talking to the Station Officer who had chided Jenny the night before.

Yes, the taxi in the affair had been confidently identified. An owner-driven beat-up unlikely to pass the inspection another year. Stolen 8.12 p.m. from outside a shelter in Pimlico. Unusual crime in the ordinary way, largely pointless. Recovered in Paulton's Square, off the King's Road.

'May I ask the nature of your interest, Mr Tucker?'

'Nicola Bland is a friend of a friend of a friend of mine.'

'I see.'

'No news of her?'

'No, sir.'

'No.'

At the moment that Colly hung up and lay back, apparently half dead, on his pillows. Nicola Bland groaned and stirred. Her eyelids twitched.

But her waking was hardly different from her sleeping. Her limbs felt immovably heavy. Her eyelids were almost too heavy to lift. And it was dark in the room. There was nothing to see – nothing worth the effort of lifting those heavy and gummy lids.

Through sleep and near-sleep and unhappy doze shot formless, gibbering things in lurid colours. There were faces which dissolved and became swirling obscenities, and spinning lime-green moons liquidly melting into mouths and fingers.

She dimly asked herself: 'What did I have too much of this time?' It did not occur to her to wonder, nor was she in any condition to wonder, where she was or why or how long she had been there.

Nigel went into Nicola's office in the afternoon – a dismal afternoon of stinging rain – an office which she had shared with a gaunt young designer with a spade-shaped beard. He fiddled with the things on her desk – an ashtray in the form of a hand, broken and glued together; chewed pencils, chewed by her pointed teeth; ball-points and felt-pens, some half-typed sheets, some handwritten scrawls, the bits and pieces of her working day – her last – yesterday.

Nigel's heart turned over and over as he stood looking at the busy litter on the desk.

In the evening Sandro took Colly to an auction at Sotheby's. A major Post-Impressionist sale, dinner-jacketed, televised.

'Some of these pictures are pretty terrible,' said Colly.

'But some are good. Some will be expensive. They expect a new record for Gauguin. And there is a Matisse which I like.'

Colly looked at the Matisse. A big, flamboyant *fauve* painting, two girls with guitars in front of a flowered backdrop.

'I know this one,' said Colly. 'I know the guy who owns it.'

'So.'

'He loves it. He loves it better than his own pink toes.'

'So,' said Sandro. 'Money is also nice.'

'He has so much he's *bored*. Why—in—hell would he be selling?'

Sandro shrugged. 'Texan?'

'Minnesotan. Now New Yorker.'

'Same thing. Fashion. Someone tells him Matisse is no longer chic. What are the motives of ignorant millionaires?'

'Matt Warren is not ignorant. This is very damned odd.'

'Hush. Attend.'

The auction was about to begin. The gossip-columns of two continents could have been (and the next day were) filled with the invited audience. Diamonds and pink pates alternated, in row upon luscious row.

Lots came and went quickly – Seurat, Braque, two small Picassos, suavely and expertly auctioned, knocked down to dealers buying for American museums.

The big Matisse came up. The bidding started at a high figure. The competition settled down, presently, to a French dealer, a well-known London dealer, and an American who was thought to be bidding for himself.

The price grew. All three seemed determined. The dealers virtually had blank checks from their principals; the American was doubtless taking advantage of United States tax legislation.

This was the sort of battle which fills auction rooms with that excited hush which has an undertone of ceaseless buzz. The bidding went jerkily – fast runs up through the thousands, the auctioneer's head clicking from side to side to pick up the nods of the bidders: then hanging, hanging, until you thought the world must have run out of money.

Great for Matt Warren, thought Colly. But why in hell is he selling?

The Frenchman dropped out. A group of Frenchmen, their tender national susceptibilities outraged by this defeat, got up and left.

This enabled Sandro and Colly to see the American bidder for the first time.

Colly knew him. Slightly. Had met him in somebody else's club. Had forgotten his name.

But would not forget that great intellectual head, the domed skull under the stiff grey thatch of hair.

The American got the picture. The price was short of a record but it was very, very high. There was a scatter of applause.

'It will go to a suitable home, I think,' said Sandro, nodding towards the successful bidder.

'Yeah. I can't remember if the guy's a professor or what. Goddam *rich,* professor.'

'A very pleased professor,' said Sandro.

It was true that the man with the lion-like grey head was accepting muted congratulations like a conqueror returned from an honourable war.

'Yeah,' said Colly. 'Taking almost indecent pleasure.'

'That is how it should be.'

'Maybe. But *gloating*, chum.'

'It is a picture to gloat over. So your friend should not be so sad.'

'Oh, he'll be sad. That's the puzzle, Sandro. I have to know the answer to something so goddam impossible.'

'I'm getting married to this thing,' said Colly, looking at the telephone with loathing.

Sandro had taken him to Flavia's rented mausoleum. Jenny was expected shortly. Flavia disapproved of Colly as strongly as anyone, and much more outspokenly than most.

Colly thought for a little, then decided on the best person to ring up. A man who knew Matt Warren well, and knew just enough about Colly not to suspect him of idle curiosity.

This man said Matt Warren had already sold a Renoir and two small Guardis.

'Tired of art?'

'I wouldn't think so.'

'Tired of those paintings?'

'You couldn't be. They're magnificent, all of them.'

'Listen,' said Colly to his distant friend. 'If Matt Warren was being blackmailed, what could it be for?'

'Well. The idea's ridiculous. Unthinkable. Well. Nothing financially bluey, that's certain. He's absolutely honest. Christ, he's too *vain* to cheat.'

'Check. I'd guess the same.'

'Girls he likes.'

'Are you sure girls?'

'Oh yes. Girls he likes, but this is a very prominent guy, Colly, with an awful lot at stake. Consequently I doubt if he's put a foot out of line in twenty years. Also very happily married, also two fine kids. Unless . . . '

'Yeah?'

'Scotch he likes.'

'He just might have got tanked and screwed someone he shouldn't?'

'He might, but . . . What the devil are we talking about? The whole idea's unthinkable.'

'Sure. Forget it.'

Colly hung up. 'You don't pay out a fortune for being caught screwing,' he said at last. 'If someone put the bite on him for that, a guy of his type would go to the police. The police would be discreet because he's rich enough to be goddam powerful. If there was publicity he'd hate it but he'd weather it. Millionaires screw people all the time, just like anybody else. He doesn't have to resign from his golf club.'

'Unless there is more.'

'Yeah. A little girl, a kid. That would be statutory rape and he'd risk a stretch. Or an accident. Jesus, what has the guy done?'

Colly looked ready to drop off to sleep, but he made another call which established the size of Matt Warren's fortune. At least his fortune until recently. It made the sale of a picture entirely unnecessary. Unless.

Jenny came in during Colly's second conversation. Her cheeks were pink from the cold of the street. Colly and Sandro both looked at her with unconcealed lust and she looked back at them with love and friendliness.

'You know a thought I think?' she said as Colly hung up. 'The *money* old pin-head must be spending.'

'Yes? Who is this extravagant?'

'Our chum. Nicola's. At least five men on the payroll. A ticket to America for something Colly says America's full of. Which I quite see it must be. Comes over here himself. There must be some fantastic great pay-off.'

Sandro and Colly both leant forward, listening. 'Go on, *carina*.'

'Well, it seems to me there are two serious possibilities. One, it's a rich man's nasty hobby. I sort of picture a nut with an obsessive desire to inflict the ultimate humiliation on gently-nurtured English birdies. Horrid theory, isn't it? Or, second, it's commercial. He's getting his money back, and with a profit. Now – big question – how do you make really big loot with a girl? Not just hiring the poor little thing out to people. The answer that makes most sense to me is —'

'Blackmail,' said Sandro.

'Nuts,' said Colly. 'The connection's impossible.'

'The connection is entirely possible,' said Sandro. 'This is not even coincidence, *caro*. Think – the timing is exactly right.'

'Accident, bite on Warren. Accident, replacement needed.'

'And only one.'

'Jesus,' said Colly. 'I better talk to Matt Warren.'

'Can you still lift the telephone, darling?'

'No. So I'll have to take a trip and talk to him personally.'

Jenny went off to her final stint at The Joint. Soon, as she expected, she saw Nigel Heywood. He seemed to be having no fun at all.

She waved at him, and then became busy with hock and Chablis and cheap claret.

When she had time, when it was late and quiet, she went to his table and sat down.

She put her hand on his and squeezed it. 'Poor love.'

'I don't believe those bloody police have any idea even where to start.'

'No, pet. I'm afraid none of us do.'

'They tried Tamara with the Identikit. Apparently it was hopeless.'

'She may be short-sighted.'

'She's just dim. Why,' he wailed, 'why Nicola and not Tamara?'

'Why? . . . How could an inch of height matter? A tiny difference of accent – really it's too bizarre . . . And then forearms. Pin-pricks.'

'What?' said Nigel.

'Tamara doesn't, I swear. Does Nicola, ever?'

'Does she what?' said Nigel, his face becoming careful.

'Make with a hypodermic?'

'No!' he said loudly. 'Sorry to shout – but no! Of course not. She may have tried pot. *Possibly* LSD.'

'Avid for sensation,' murmured Jenny. 'But truly and honestly no pins and needles.'

'Absolutely not.'

'Oh dear. We'd better have some more brandy. I don't say it'll *help,* but it'll be comforting.'

Jenny herself tried to be comforting, only she had no comfort to offer. She saw that Nigel found it painful to talk about Nicola; she guessed he found it even more painful not to; agony to talk uselessly on and on, round and round the strangeness of the affair, but a greater agony not to.

At last he was tired: blessedly groggy: and he left.

He was wearing a short macintosh instead of his long navy-blue overcoat, and he had left his hat in his office; he was not recognised by the man in the parked Vauxhall or his friend nearby who had been watching the door of The Joint since seven o'clock.

Jenny was.

She had taken affectionate farewell of the manager, pulled on some trousers and the skin of the unknown shaggy animal, and emerged into the Fulham Road. There were a few people about: very few. She walked east for half a mile looking for a taxi (her Mini was already under repair, in a small discreet Kensington garage). She was glad to let the cold wet wind blow the brandy and the smell of the restaurant out of her head.

She found a taxi and lay back in the seat and lit a cigarette.

Something nagged at the back of her mind. Something had been odd.

About Nigel? No. About The Joint? Someone in The Joint? She thought not. About the street? Something in the street?

Lots of odd things happened late at night in the Fulham Road. It would never do to get nervy. Sandro would not be sympathetic; Nicola would not be found.

She peered through the rear window. The taxi was not being followed.

Oh well. And she was tired.

She stopped the cab in front of Moss Bros. There was no need for it to thread the little alleys to her door. And it was not now raining hard.

Paying off the taxi was a noisy business, as always. The door clanged shut; the flag on the meter clanged up; the taxi's engine ticked over with the noise of an alert fire-engine; when it drove off the engine thudded like a foreign train.

Jenny shivered and pulled her shaggy old coat close round her. She turned the corner by Moss Bros and started her short cold walk.

She suddenly realised what had struck her as odd.

A man had gone into a telephone box just after she emerged into the Fulham Road.

Normal enough.

But he had been waiting by the box. Leaning against it.

Not normal.

Jenny smelled danger, immediate, imminent, very close, very bad. Her antennae were schooled to intense sensitivity by other risks in other places; now they prickled and twitched.

She guessed she was being followed.

They did see the car number, then.

This was all because of the slipper.

The early fruit lorries had not yet started their shunting, grinding, roaring and banging. The little streets were dead quiet except for the tick-tock of Jenny's boot-heels (not hurrying, not dawdling) on the wet asphalt.

Jenny was frightened.

She thought it would be a knife. But a gun was possible.

5

Jenny walked on (not hurrying, not dawdling) making a plan, senses vividly alert, antennae vibrating.

Twenty yards to go to the corner where she turned left. Then ten yards to her door, on the right.

Dim light from a single street-lamp a little ahead. Stinging rain. Execution weather.

A dark flicker, almost too quick and dark to see – the swirl of the skirts of a coat. A man just round the corner, waiting for her.

The single street-lamp was two yards off. Jenny walked on, three unhurried strides, and stopped dead.

A faint rustle and rattle behind her. Yes, another behind and quite close.

It would be natural if, now, she groped for her latch-key. But it was all a question of time.

Jenny reached deep into her trouser pocket and found her heavy gold cigarette-lighter. She struggled her hand out again, through the heavy constricting clothes she wore. Her spine tingled. Any second a thrown knife could spike indifferently through the shaggy leather, the wool, the soft pink skin of her back.

She freed her hand, holding the heavy little lump of precious metal. She hoped very hard she could throw straight. She threw.

She threw very straight. The lighter smashed the street-lamp and its bulb and the dark street was pitch-dark.

There were no lit windows here, no shops, no cars, no lights at all.

Jenny flattened herself instantly against the cold wall of the warehouse on her left. Something whistled past her, inches away. It clanged against an outcrop of wall and rattled metallically to the street.

A knife, breast-high, accurately thrown to where she had been.

He'd have at least two. And there was at least one other man.

Jenny shrugged off her pale-coloured fur. Their eyes would very soon get accustomed to the not-quite-total darkness. The fur slithered silently to the street. She stepped out of her short woolly boots, using the coat to muffle the sound. She could just see the coat, a blur at her feet.

Her trousers and sweater were dark and she wore a dark headscarf.

Barefooted (and it was horribly cold and wet) she slipped across the narrow street.

Footsteps thudded. Someone lit a match; Jenny got a glimpse of a gingery, hairy face. He got a glimpse of her coat. One of them picked it up. Her boots fell on to the pavement. They swore. They lit more matches.

'Get the car, Roddy. Quick.'

Footsteps rattled away.

Car. Headlights. Maybe a spotlight.

'She must be in this street still. Murch, stay that end. Cobb, this corner.'

More hurrying, obedient footsteps.

Jenny was bottled up. Light was coming, lots of it, blazing, making the bare little street as helpful to hide in as a white-tiled prison cell.

Jenny had given one huge, shuddering sigh of relief when her lighter had providentially hit the street-lamp. Now she was very frightened again.

The car must be near. The light would come very soon. Her feet were wet and cold and she was shivering with fright and with cold.

She had walked down this little featureless street hundreds of times in the months she had had the flat; but it was not pretty or interesting and she had hardly looked at it. High blank walls, almost windowless. Hardly a door.

Jenny tried furiously to remember if there was anything she could climb up or any hole she could crawl into.

Roddy, Murch, Cobb and their whiskery leader presumably knew the street even less well. Was there anything to know?

Jenny visualised, concentrating, shivering. In her mind's eye she saw only the high, blank walls in the dirty yellow of London brick. No drain-pipes, no bolt-holes, the windows small and high, the few doorways shallow and useless. The only thing was the street-lamp.

Jenny clamped her jaws together to stop her teeth chattering. She longed for Sandro's help and his strength and his gun. She longed to be somewhere quite different.

She stood still and listened. Opposite, by the street-lamp, a man coughed and shifted his feet.

The hurrying footsteps had stopped. Both ends of the street were guarded. It was narrow enough for one man to guard even in the dark.

It would not be dark long. A self-starter was whirring not far away, clearly audible. In a second the engine would fire and the lights would be switched on, and then very soon she would be dead.

The self-starter still whirred. The engine would be damp and cold.

'Sod,' said the invisible man opposite.

Two things happened at once.

The engine of the car fired, and light glowed at the far end of the little street, the beam at right-angles to the street. The car had to move forward a short distance and turn.

And the man under the street-lamp strode away towards the car. He had rubber soles. They squeaked on the wet street and his coat rustled.

Jenny sped across the street again and started to climb the lamp-post. It was not high enough to be safe for her, even at the top, but it might lead somewhere.

It was all there was.

Jenny could climb like a cat, having spent a large part of her childhood in the upper branches of trees. But this lamp-post was horrible to climb. It was cold to her hands and her bare feet, and the rain made it slippery. She wrapped her legs round it and hauled herself up, trying to be quick and being agonisingly slow, fighting her way up the slippery hateful metal. She began to breathe harshly with effort and with fright. She began to be frightened that her breath could be heard.

The car engine was being revved. They would move at any moment.

Jenny got near the top of the lamp-post and there was a crossbar. She heaved herself up more easily by the crossbar and got a knee over it.

As she groped upwards again her hand was suddenly and shockingly hurt. She sucked in her breath sharply with the pain and she nearly lost her grip and fell.

The lamp had been on for hours. It had only just gone off. It was blazing hot.

Gripping with her arms and knees, Jenny pulled the sleeves of her sweater down to cover her hands. She groped upwards again. She found she could bear contact with the hot metal briefly through the protecting wool – but only briefly.

She managed to get into a precarious crouch on the crossbar, half embracing the hot lamp. Something cracked and tinkled under her hands.

Broken glass.

Jenny sobbed with effort and terror.

The car was moving now. The glow from its headlights strengthened.

They had not really been slow. Danger bends the time-scale.

Jenny could now see, dimly, the wall beside her.

She thought the men would look up soon, but not straight away.

On the wall she could see a long, narrow, vertical wooden sign: some vegetable wholesaler's sign – old, shabby, solid. It reached up to the gutter.

Jenny very gingerly stretched her legs. When she could no longer keep her balance on the crossbar she let her weight fall towards the wall. It was a little further than she expected. She whimpered at the thought of falling. Her feet nearly slipped.

Leaning on the wall with both hands, she found she could reach the wooden sign. But she would have to climb higher up the lamp-post before she could get on to the sign.

She had to put her bare feet on to the hot metal lid of the street-lamp.

She gritted her teeth and stepped up on to it, clawing up the wooden sign with her hands. The pain on the soles of her feet was bad.

There were bolts and brackets at intervals holding the sign to the wall. She got a footing quite easily. Then she climbed quickly and safely to the top.

The car was in the street now. Its headlights raked the asphalt and the yellowish brick walls.

Jenny grabbed for the gutter and got her elbows on to it.

She had to swing her weight far out over the street to get past the gutter. It was bad, but no worse than some of the trees (and gutters) of her childhood.

Then she was on the roof.

Her feet hurt. The broken glass had cut her arms and legs and torn her clothes. She had grazed her elbows and hurt her hands on the gutter. She tried to control her rasping breaths. Her heart thudded in her throat.

The car crawled down the street in bottom gear. She could hear footsteps and murmurs.

They would realise about the lamp-post, though they would

find it difficult to believe. She doubted if any of them would be able to follow her up, and she was sure she could cope with a single attacker coming over the gutter. But they could find another way up. They could break down a door and get on to the roof from inside.

It was dark and wet and cold on the roof and the wind gusted at her viciously. Jenny kept her eyes away from the light in the street below so that she could see in the dark. She was exhausted and very sore.

She slithered up the roof to the ridge, then crawled along to the next building which was flat-roofed and a little higher. She climbed on to this and could walk to its far side. There a drain-pipe led to a fire-escape and in seconds she was in another street and running.

She found a taxi in the Strand and asked for Eaton Square.

The driver looked oddly at her bare feet, her torn trousers and the smears of blood on her arms and face. She showed him a pound note. (It was lucky she had her wages from The Joint.) Reluctantly he let her into his cab.

She wanted a cigarette very badly. But she had no lighter. The cab-driver said he was a non-smoker. There would be matches in Eaton Square.

Flavia was sitting up in bed, in her palatial but characterless hired bedroom. She was swathed in apricot silk. She was wearing glasses, and reading a slim but expensive book called *Investment Analysis: How To Get Better-Than-Average Growth Without The Speculative Element: A New Philosophy.* She made notes on a little gold pad with a little gold pencil.

Sandro, as a matter of politeness, had demanded entry; Flavia had laughed and refused. He was sitting in the drawing room, in a very well-cut dark blue suit from Sackville Street, a shirt from Jermyn Street, shoes from St James's Street, and a tie from the Rue de Rivoli. He was reading a highly confidential Brazilian government publication which examined, statistically, the effect of certain stimulant drugs on the stamina and bravado of habitual criminals. He was frightened by what he read, and by the thought of the organisers of violent crime staffing their operations with fearless, souped-up zombies.

Colly, in another armchair, seemed to be not so much asleep as under hypnosis. He stared vacantly at a fly which orbited interminably round a lamp.

He was fishing out, from his very good memory, the names and circumstances of recent suicides of very rich men. There were three. All of them were to an extent a puzzle: causeless or inadequately caused. None of the three men had incurable diseases or wrecked marriages. All of them could have been blackmail victims who couldn't take any more.

Blackmail was probably the likeliest answer for them all. But then the coincidence would be incredible. Unless it was no coincidence but the working of a single racket.

A racket which would have to be expensive and well organised.

Three suicides. That's where it ended with big-time blackmail. Disgrace and ruin if you didn't pay. Simple ruin if you did pay. You were caught in a jam with no way out, no way out at all. So you took a dive.

How many more? Was Matt Warren reaching this point?

The doorbell rang discreetly. Discreet feet shuffled to answer it. There was a pause full of murmured dismay and reluctance.

'Don't think I don't *realise* I'm not dressed for the Ritz,' said a high, clear, well-loved voice.

'Jenny!' roared Sandro and Colly in unison.

'Darling, they're very properly doubting if I'm quite what you want to see—'

The butler, with gloom and doubt on his face, opened the drawing room door and Jenny was allowed in.

Sandro sighed.

'Don't tell me,' he said. 'Let me guess. You have been to *a bal masque* in the amusing costume of a street-arab. No? Then someone has tried to murder you.' He yelled: 'Flavia!'

'There's no need to bother Flavia,' said Jenny.

'Of course not, but she is a rich man's Florence Nightingale. Is that a good English joke?'

'Sick,' said Colly, whose eyes were half closed again but who was looking at Jenny with concern and excitement.

Flavia swept in, took one look at Jenny, and gave a little scream of horror and pleasure.

'Darling Jen, how *horrible*. But how *lovely* to see you. They been running you over? Why can't you people behave?'

Flavia almost carried Jenny into the padded perfections of her bathroom, and then bathed her cuts and grazes and anointed her burns.

'Honey,' she said, dabbing gently and expertly at the sore parts of Jenny's person (as she had a few years ago dabbed, cooing, at the sore parts of her younger brothers and sisters), 'honey, what *have* you been doing?'

'*Too* squalid. *Quite* awful. This man who was giving me dinner, simply creepy—'

'Why go out with a creep?'

'It's all life. The rich tapestry. Warp, woof, weft, weave—'

'What you mean is, you date a heel just for kicks?'

'Don't be severe when I'm lacerated.'

'You and Sandro. I'm a hick, thank God, but some things I do know.'

'Peasant cunning, love.'

'It keeps me out of this kind of rape situation.'

'He never. Try as he might.'

'What did he try with? A blow torch?'

'Weft, wharf, whoop – it sounds like something you might shout to a Welsh foxhound.'

'I despise bloodsports,' said Flavia.

She lent Jenny pyjamas and a robe, too large for her, and they came back into the drawing room.

'A different *bal masque*,' said Sandro. 'I see you are now Christopher Robin.'

'I feel like Piglet,' said Jenny, 'small and scared.'

'That is something we should discuss.'

Flavia went back to bed and resumed the financial education which she needed much less than many Wall Street brokers.

'So?' said Sandro.

'They got the car number. They were waiting outside the flat.'

'Then you must not go near the flat until they are all dead or locked up.'

'No. Such a bore. And the dogs are there.'

'Colly will get the dogs,' said Sandro.

'Hey,' said Colly. 'No.'

'No. On second thoughts there is no reason they should be allowed to link any of us yet.'

'Somebody must get them,' said Jenny. 'They'll want a drink, and breakfast tomorrow. And a walk. I mean, my eiderdown . . '

'We will fix something. Your uncles will fix. Meanwhile you must disappear.'

'Not forever, Sandro pet.'

'Just so. Therefore we must consider how to destroy these rude people.'

'Where did our rest go?' mumbled Colly. 'That vacation? Do you go to the cops about tonight, Jenny?'

'They'll be vexed if I don't. Roddy, Murch, Cobb and the gingery man.'

'The gingery guy they know about.'

'Yes. So now we have those names.'

'No faces? No voices?'

'They must do what they can with the names. Goodness, how tired I am. Sandro pet, can Flavia give me a bed?'

'A thousand.'

Jenny yawned. 'So late again. The dogs will be wondering where I am.'

'You would be best going abroad for a few days until we make a plan.'

'You choose, love. Somewhere warm.'

'I'll come too,' said Colly.

'You have work,' said Sandro.

Colly groaned.

The police were called. A glum detective made a note of the names Roddy, Murch and Cobb. Another detective had heard of a Murch, but believed him to be in Parkhurst. They agreed that Jenny should not return to her flat. They consented to take her dogs and deliver them to her home in the country. They had no idea what was going on or who was responsible.

Early in the morning (film-makers' hours) Flavia May left her front door in Eaton Square and got into the back seat of a Studio Humber. She was followed out of the house and into the car by a secretary or companion – a downtrodden young woman in dark glasses, enveloped in a macintosh, with a lot of untidy dark hair which might have been a wig.

The Humber went northwards, by St John's Wood and the A5.

'Jen, your rapist must be a very determined guy,' said Flavia, as bright and disapproving in the morning as at night.

'Terrifying,' said Jenny. 'Mad.'

'Can't you get police protection?'

'And walk about all day with a bluebottle fore and aft?' and me looking for a job?'

'If you think you'll get a job with that carpet on your head you're crazy.'

'Actually I think I'll rest for a bit.'

'Your life,' said Flavia drily, 'is so horribly exhausting.'

Flavia was headed for a studio in the northern suburbs, where she was to meet the lighting-cameraman into whose hands she would shortly be committing responsibility for her beauty. In a patch of wooded country near Boreham wood she told the chauffeur to stop. Jenny got out.

'You'll be okay, darling?'

'A-okay. A chum will whizz up any second.'

Flavia nodded. She blew Jenny a kiss through the rear window as the Humber accelerated away.

Jenny sat under a tree a little way back from the road. She drew her knees up under her chin and smoked three cigarettes. It was cold and clear, with a light north-east wind.

'No similar recent cases.' But she was nagged by an elusive memory. Something had happened, something she knew about, which pre-echoed these unpleasant events.

She worried at this shadow at the very edge of her mind. She tried to grab it and hold it up to the light; it danced away, hiding its face. She decided that the more she chased it the faster it ran away. She would have to let it come, and then pounce.

She lit a fourth cigarette. The memory of something important, something relevant, something (she thought) hushed-up and nasty mocked her from the periphery of consciousness.

At eight-thirty an M.G.B. drew up a hundred yards away and Nigel Heywood got out. He was correctly dressed for the country, in tweeds and a cap. Jenny rose and walked to meet him.

'Now what?' said Nigel. 'My God you rang me up early.'

'It seemed beadiest,' said Jenny. 'Are you ill?'

'What?'

'I mean, what do you tell your office?'

'Oh, yes, not well at all. Look, what is all this? Why me?'

'You're involved, pet. We thought you'd be the one to help.'

'Mm,' said Nigel non-committally.

They got into the car and Nigel drove, at Jenny's direction, down on to the M4 and westwards.

They came at last, beyond Salisbury, to a countryside of rivers and rich valleys.

'What do you and your friends think?' asked Nigel after a long silence. 'What is all this?'

'We think it must be the edge of something quite big. There must be a *point*, and there do seem to be so many *people*.'

'This Sandro – is he some kind of boyfriend of yours?'
'Yes and no. I foam with adoration for him. Yes and no.'
'Colleague?'
'And that. That, more.'
'In what, exactly?'
'Oh, I suppose you'll see.'
'Will I?'
'Nicola.'
'Yes,' said Nigel nervously. 'How the hell did you get involved?'
'*Force majeure.* And via Sandro.'
'How on earth did you link up with him?'
'We met in Italy,' said Jenny. 'He was a friend of friends.'
She said no more, but her mind raced back to the blood-spattered evening eighteen months before. . .

For her twentieth birthday, Jenny's quirkish and unapproachable great-uncle the Duke of Sturminster gave her the return fare to Milan. It was August. She stayed near Como with Italian cousins of country neighbours of her parents. It was pleasant and uneventful – bathing, sailing, canasta, a little Milanese culture, and a few parties of pulverising grandness and great tedium. The last of these parties outdid the others in grandness and promised to outdo them in boredom: until dinner (for thirty-four, eaten off gold plate) was interrupted by six masked men with submachine-guns who removed gold, silver, jewellery and four small priceless pictures. Two servants and one guest, who showed token resistance, were shot dead. While Jenny herself was being robbed of diamond earrings and a small rope of pearls her despoiler's mask slipped. She – only she – glimpsed his face. There was a muttered conference among the gang, in which the decision to kill her was unmistakably taken. At this point a powerful, rather ugly Italian, to whom she had barely been introduced, got her out of the room and away over the rooftops to safety. After various hectic episodes and several more deaths she could once again go safely into the streets. She even got her necklace back.

In the course of these events she came to admire and trust her rescuer as no one else.

'A friend of friends,' she repeated to Nigel. 'We get on rather cosily. Added to which,' she went on obscurely, 'I always wanted to be a boy . . .

A giant beech in the home park. Well-hidden ropes. At the top, hammocks and stale provisions and a Victorian first-aid kit. Jenny, seven, eight and nine years old, becoming Midshipman J. Norrington in command of the forepeak. Sometimes she was Captain; sometimes Bloody Norrington, the pirate feared throughout the Spanish main for his daring and his brutality. She cut off her own hair with the nursery scissors, to the scandal of her Nanny.

For a time, in other trees, she was Lieutenant J. Norrington of the Hussars (or the Rajput Lancers, or the Heavy Dragoons) or a Colonel, or a drummer-boy.

She tried never, never to cry.

'So when I found myself doing quite *stern and manly* things with Sandro,' she said to Nigel as they hummed across another little river, 'it was the *most* dreamlike wish-fulfilment thing.'

'Good God,' said Nigel.

'And then, you see, it's like smoking.'

Like drugs, like alcohol.

'Won't you ever settle down?' asked her aunts. Mothers of other daughters, who resented her beauty, clucked at her fecklessness and secretly rejoiced. 'You must feel it's time,' they cooed to her mother, 'that Jennifer settled down.'

They meant: poor girl, unsatisfactory daughter, no steady Second Secretary, or lord of large acreages, or brewing or banking scion. They meant: what a shaming succession of unserious jobs, what a thumb-twiddling day-to-day life.

Had they known about the time she killed, by burning, a man

called Rocco il Porco, they would have screamed.

As had Rocco il Porco.

'Through there,' said Jenny. 'There may be a few holes in the drive.'

Nigel turned between Jacobean lodges and drove cautiously up a drive which was, in fact, in excellent order. They trundled over a cattle-grid. Deer (the famous black herd) flicked between the elms and oaks and beeches of the park. The house was quite soon visible, though still a long way away – delicate Georgian Gothic on a monumental scale, rebuilt by a pupil of Nicholas Hawkesmoor in 1740. The Norringtons were fortunately still very rich.

'Wow,' said Nigel, who was by no means past being impressed by the aristocracy.

'Very cosy and dilapidated in bits,' said Jenny. 'The garden invades quite a lot of it.'

'I can imagine, fabulous orchids from the hot-houses.'

'Yes, rather sexy and terrifying. But I mean worm-casts appearing in the drawing room carpet and molehills popping up in the Gents. Sandro's house is the grand one. No worm would dare show its face there.'

She thought about Sandro, who was fixing the second stage of her disappearance. She expected he would send her to Italy.

Sandro, since he was writing her name for a travel agent, was thinking about Jenny.

He had despised her at their first meeting, in the huge Uccello *salone*. A pink-and-white Anglo-Saxon, a lightweight Flavia. It had none the less seemed a good thing to seize a small opportunity to save her life when she was about to be filled with soft-nosed bullets from a stolen machine-pistol. Thereafter, for some weeks, saving her life and his own took on the quality of an absorbing and guilty game.

To his very great surprise this little, soft, over-protected, ill-read bit of fluff turned out to be ruthless and resourceful. Nothing shocked her. She was often frightened but always dangerous. She was clever, a quality which Sandro, who was clever, never under-valued. He came to adore her.

And Sandro himself?

He knew that psychologists said of obsessive gamblers that they underwent the agonies of suspense and loss in order to deaden for themselves the pang of some greater pain. This had been his state: but for gambling read the fear of death – read the game of chess where pawns are lives and checkmate is final indeed . . .

The travel agent nodded and made notes. Il Conte would receive confirmation and a typed itinerary for Her Ladyship.

'Still cold out there, I hear.'

'The camellias will soon be out,' said Sandro with nostalgia.

Nigel stopped in front of an enormous portico and felt alarmed. He had no intimate experience of this sort of thing. He wondered if his palm would sweat.

Jenny's total and unquestioning assurance was suddenly explained. She had come out into the world from *that* door.

'Come on, love,' said Jenny. 'Nice drive, thank you. Let's have a drink.'

A thin, good-looking lady of fifty crossed the gravel (acres of gravel) towards them. She wore a macintosh and gumboots and carried a pitchfork. Wisps of hay clung to her hair.

'Why do we need fourteen donkeys? What good do they do?' she said fiercely to Nigel.

'They're sweet. Hullo, Ma,' said Jenny.

Mother and daughter embraced warmly. The Countess of Teffont still held her pitchfork.

Jenny had taken off her wig; she held it as she kissed her mother.

'I see, darling, that you have just scalped an immigrant.'

'He was *pestering* me, Ma.'

'Then I dare say you did the only possible thing.' She turned to Nigel, smiled cautiously, and held out a hand. Her eyes were startling: Jenny's eyes.

'Nigel Heywood,' said Jenny.

'How do you do?' said Nigel.

'How nice of you to come. I *suppose* there's lunch. All fourteen wretched donkeys have had more hay than I thought there was in the world. It *looks* so light,' she said sternly to Nigel, 'and it turns out to be so heavy. How I resent being deceived.'

'Why can't Chapman feed your donkeys?' asked Jenny. 'Groom,' she explained to Nigel.

'Such a *snob*. And ten hunters now, heaven knows why. Miserable animals stick to us like glue.' She turned to Nigel again. 'Don't you find that? Turn your back for one single second, and when you turn round again, more animals have joined you.'

'Can you manage my dogs for a bit?' said Jenny. 'I might be going away.'

'Lupin, Geranium, Poppy, Calvados, and what are those puppies called?'

'Too silly. Somerville and Ross.'

'Of course, darling, lovely to have them. They can sleep with the pugs in the Gents. Oh,' said Lady Teffont, 'I'm dead with cold and fatigue.'

'Me too,' said Nigel.

'We'll all find a warming drink.'

They went in. There were no worm-casts on the drawing room carpet, which was a little larger than a tennis court.

Roddy, Murch, Cobb and a fourth man were thirty-five miles away and travelling briskly.

6

Jenny's father joined them for lunch: a gentle-mannered man of sixty who liked surprising his neighbours, whose occasional speeches in the House of Lords were too academic for most of his fellow-peers to understand, and who in the previous season had been fourth in the list of winning racehorse owners. He cultivated eccentricity to hide his toughness; he had nearly doubled the large fortune his father left him. He had spent the morning rubbing ointment into a labrador, writing a vitriolic letter, in German, to a Swiss botanical periodical, arranging nominations to stallions for some of his brood-mares, trying a dozen dry-flies of his own pattern (a body dubbed of pekingese-fur with a gold twist, a dark blue bantam-hackle) and buying, by telephone, a controlling interest in a firm of city wine-merchants.

He asked Nigel, with convincingly simulated interest, where he had been at school.

'School,' said Jenny softly.

'A word,' said her father affectionately, 'which I gravely doubt if you can even spell, you grubby little illiterate.'

The elusive memory Jenny had chased in the morning was suddenly pinned on a big white board in her mind. It was necessary to check up on it at once.

'I must visit Wapshott Castle,' she said.

'To what end? To enrol yourself again? You were not a success five years ago.'

'It's only twenty miles. Nigel, will you take me?'

'Of course,' said Nigel, mystified but anxious to please.

'Is that why you came?' said Lord Teffont. 'To visit your dear old Coll?'

'No,' said Jenny. 'This is a scheme which I have this very second hatched.'

'Then why did you come, darling?' asked her mother.

'To pack, Ma. Clothes for warmer climes.'

'How lovely it would be if just occasionally we had the least idea what you were doing.'

'I'm a big girl now.'

'Yes, such a shame.'

After lunch Jenny packed a few clothes for Italy (she assumed Sandro would send her to Italy) and they left in Nigel's car by the back drive.

They passed the buildings of the home farm and the neat rectangle of the stud. In a white-railed paddock a group of disconsolate barren mares were being allowed to enjoy the frosty sunshine.

'Poor loves,' said Jenny. 'Probably the stallions' fault.'

Between a field of winter wheat and a hillside planted with young larch Jenny had a sudden and deeply disquieting thought.

'I wonder if we're not being terribly stupid. So far their intelligence has been pretty good.'

'What?'

'They linked me with that bloody slipper via my car number. They didn't take long finding my flat. Two more seconds with a reference book and they know this is where I live.'

'Yes.'

'They want to kill us. So we must assume they'll come here.'

'If you're not here does it matter? They won't assassinate the household.'

'But, love, I am here. Suppose they started early, rightly guessing where I'd come today. Suppose they looked at the map. Dropped a couple of gentlemen at each lodge. Let's think.

We can't assume they never have guns. Would they expect me to leave? More to hole up safely in the cellarage, guarded by mastiffs . . . Rifles with telescopic sights is what I'd have, if I was them. Oh dear. They might shoot a maid. We shall have to draw them off or something.'

Nigel looked frightened. But he obediently turned the car and drove back past the stud and the barns and cowsheds.

Jenny tried to think what the enemy would do. She imagined rifles behind the farm buildings. These people were ruthless. They had a lot at stake. It was not yet clear what it was they had at stake; it was clear that it was a lot. Rifles behind the farm buildings were possible. They were even probable.

'Faster,' she said to Nigel.

Soon they rolled into the huge paved yard behind the West Wing. Dogs barked at them cheerfully from kennels; other dogs slobbered over them; Old English game bantams stalked about like dandies in a disorganised minuet.

They went through a small door and along miles of stone passage. Larder, still-room, bakery, creamery, laundry; then, nearer the heart of the house, flower-room, rod-room, gun-room, a dog-room or two. They came at last, by a baize-covered door, into the domed immensity of the hall, which was floored by a Roman mosaic plundered from a dig in Tunisia in 1880.

A black 3-8 Jaguar (property of a Lewisham estate agent, as it happened, who was wondering what his son had done with it) had just drawn up. Two nondescript men got out of the back and wandered idly away in different directions. The driver stayed where he was. A fourth man came to the front door, and a bell boomed along the stone passages.

The man at the door had a broad, pink, shiny face and a bald skull. He looked as though he had been shaven too close, by a keen apprentice barber, a few minutes before.

Huxtable, the butler, could be heard ponderously approaching.

'Oh dear,' murmured Jenny. 'Too late. I ought to have briefed Huxtable.' She pulled Nigel into an alcove behind a tapestry screen.

'Good afternoon,' said Huxtable at the door, his voice rising with a stately note of interrogation.

'I have an urgent message,' said the shiny man, 'for Lady Jennifer Norrington.'

'I'm afraid, sir, that Her Ladyship has this moment left.'

'*She was here?*'

'Yes, sir, for luncheon.'

'*Where has she gone?*'

'May I ask, sir, who wishes to know?'

'Of course, old boy,' said naked-face bluffly. 'Quite right to check.' He produced a note-case with a cellophane window. 'Sergeant Reilly, Salisbury C.I.D.'

The card must have looked genuine, at least to Huxtable. Jenny guessed it was genuine.

'Will you come in, Sergeant?'

'No thanks, old boy. Just tell me which way Lady Jennifer went.'

Nigel glanced at Jenny, small and silent beside him. He was surprised to see that she had a gun in her hand.

'Her Ladyship,' said Huxtable, 'announced her intention of visiting Wapshott Castle. A school. Thank you, Sergeant.'

This name had a visible, though momentary, effect on the Sergeant. His face seemed to flame for an instant. He was immediately under control again. He thanked Huxtable, and in a few seconds the Jaguar spun its wheels in the gravel and rocketed away down the front drive.

'That solves one problem,' said Jenny, 'but at the same time creates new ones. Of course they're going the long way round. But quickly.'

'What we can do is go straight back to London!' said Nigel.

'No, love. I absolutely must chat to old Winnie.'

'Winnie . . . ?'

'Miss Olivia Winstanley, M.A. Cantab., teacher of history at Wapshott Castle, the greatly overpriced seminary for the daughters of the nobility and gentry.'

'We can't go there!'

'It's only twenty miles, pet.'

'But they'll be there!'

'Come along.'

As they drove, Jenny said: 'Did you recognise that bogus Sergeant?'

'No,' said Nigel. 'I don't think so. I'm not sure. Did you?'

'I'm not sure either,' said Jenny crossly. 'Vexing. If we could only tail him—'

'*Tail him?*'

'But we can't. Do go faster.'

'Here,' said Jenny, 'my local knowledge is going to be lovely and handy. I do hope I can remember.'

Nigel drove past the Victorian gates of Wapshott Castle and up a bone-rattling track of frozen and bumpy mud, and berthed the car in the lee of a tangle of yew and rhododendron.

'Loathsome shrubs,' said Jenny, 'but at least they keep their leaves.'

'Do you always carry a gun?'

'Not always. Let's think a minute. They'll have got here. They'll have asked and been told we haven't arrived. They'll wait. Where? Three of them not counting the driver. Some here, some there.'

'We can't get in!'

'Hush, love. Fright is right but panic is manic. Original, yes? Think more . . . They'll want me going in if possible, rather than coming out, if what I guess is true. The great thing is, they don't know we know they're here. Yes. It won't be difficult at all. How's your head for heights?'

'Fair.'

'It better be. Come on.'

She led Nigel through a long and winding tunnel of shrubbery.

In warmer weather it would have been boggy; even in this hard bright weather it squelched and stank.

They rounded a fallen willow, branches tangled with brambles and dead briony. Jenny gestured Nigel to caution and silence. They peered through a lattice of twigs.

The house loomed thirty yards away – a crenellated Victorian pile with whimsical towers and stained glass in some of the windows. Smart, incongruous modern additions of glass and blond wood stuck out at the flanks; there were bicycle-sheds and tennis-courts, and bleak playing fields laid out in the park beyond.

No Jaguar.

It suddenly seemed to Nigel that they were behaving like idiots. The men had gone away. They could walk up to the school and go in. He was about to say this to Jenny, in a sensible normal voice, when he suddenly smelled tobacco. Surely even Jenny, if she seriously thought they were in danger . . . He saw by her face that she smelled it too. She sniffed, turning her head. She looked like a hind on a Highland hillside, aware of danger but uncertain of its direction; and she looked like a beast of prey.

In this close woody place, and in a valley between hills, the light wind eddied and shifted. But the smoker was close.

A twig snapped, a few yards to their left front.

Jenny's face cleared. She took out her gun. Then she put it away again and took out a vicious little flexible cosh. Her movements were confident, stealthy, unhurried. Her expression was abstracted and serious: she wore no face Nigel had ever seen her wear before.

She gestured to Nigel to stay where he was, then slid without sound behind an unkempt yew. She moved slowly. The cosh hung from her wrist by a loop.

Nigel's heart pounded loudly in his throat.

He thought he heard the *chunk* of cosh on skull; he certainly heard the rustle and thud of a body falling in dense undergrowth.

Jenny was beside him again. On her face was her normal

expression of tranquil silliness.

'He didn't see my face,' she murmured. 'And I've never seen him before. We might do something with this . . . 'It was a heavy, blued revolver with a short barrel. 'Do you fancy it, love?'

Nigel recoiled and shook his head.

'Probably wise. Clumsy great thing, and they do go off with such a bang.'

She thrust it, with a small and contemptuous foot, into a muddy crevice among leaves and brambles. 'I wonder where the others are?'

'Did you kill him?'

'It *occurred* to me. I'm probably wrong, but I decided not to. So horrid for the school, stiffs all over the pleasure-grounds.'

'Would you have?'

She looked at him without expression. 'Yes, love. Come on.'

Some birches and brooms covered them to a bicycle-shed which ran up to the wall of the house.

'Here's where we creep discreetly in,' said Jenny chattily.

'How?' asked Nigel in a sick voice.

'Up. Watch. Move quick.'

Jenny slid from the oily gloom of the stacked bicycles to the base of a fat drain-pipe. She went up it like a cat and swung over the mock battlements of a squat tower.

Nigel gulped and followed. The drain-pipe was square and hurt his hands. The uneven stone of the wall made the climb quite easy, but his skin crawled with imagined firearms in the woods behind him. He climbed and climbed, hand over hand, clutching the drain-pipe, toes finding the deep gaps between the stones. The drain-pipe curved into the wall, to serve a gutter behind the battlements. There were two full feet of bare stone above its top. Nigel gulped. He was streaming with sweat in spite of the cold. A small dirty hand thrust down and caught his arm and he tumbled over the battlements on to a flat lead roof.

'I wonder who saw us? I don't think they'd watch this side at all. No doors. Anyway, the next bit's in cover.'

The next bit was a ledge at the edge of a sloping roof; it bordered a well, gaping to the left, which lit the basements.

Jenny sped across and turned and stood waiting.

Nigel started more slowly. He glanced involuntarily to his left and down: to emptiness, and to granite and concrete and glass a very long way down.

He stuck. His body swayed and his eyes swivelled. He began to tremble violently.

He felt himself somehow pulled and steered to the solidity of gently sloping leads.

His head cleared. 'Sorry,' he muttered.

'*Vertige,* pet. Nothing in the world to be ashamed of. I ought to have thought. I've done that crossing a million times, on little expeditions while I was here. In fact that's why they sort of expelled me, too humiliating. Coming back from Salisbury races. It was worth it, I made eighteen bob . . . Actually, love, I don't quite know why you're here. *Lovely* to have you, of course, but you could perfectly well have stayed in the car.'

Nigel was speechless.

Jenny led him through an open window and they jumped down into a room. It had several beds, with chests-of-drawers and teddy bears. A number of half-dressed thirteen-year-olds were changing for outdoor exercise. They screamed and giggled. Nigel eyed with interest a naked redhead who was pretending to have hysterics. Her little breasts shook; in two years' time she would be a menace.

Jenny saw this, and laughed, and pulled Nigel out into a passage.

The rickety attic stairs widened as they descended and the plasterwork became formal. The corridors grew broader and had higher ceilings.

'Will that pink man come in?' asked Nigel.

Jenny had asked herself the same question. 'I doubt it,' she said. 'On what excuse? He's banged on the door once and they told him we hadn't got here. So they'll sit and wait. They could go all stone-age and grab a few girls as hostages, but I don't think they will. They'll wait for us to come in, or if they saw us go in they'll wait for us to come out. I somehow feel they don't want a huge stink. I somehow feel their boss wouldn't like it.'

'Small-head.'

'Yes. No guns when we had our little motor-race. A niminy-piminy master criminal. How I dislike him.'

'How do we get out?'

'Good question. But premature, pet. Let's get what we came for first.'

'Which is what, for God's sake?'

'A bit of background information.'

They were now in a land of broad passages with carpets. Jenny knocked on a heavy mahogany door.

'Come in.'

Miss Winstanley was rising sixty, small, sharp-eyed, sharp-nosed. She wore a mid-calf tweed skirt and a heavy woollen twin-set. Gold-rimmed spectacles were a little askew on her nose. The arrangement of her grey hair was old-fashioned and apparently done in the dark.

She was sitting at a desk correcting exercise-books.

'Jennifer,' she said sharply, 'there is no reason for you to come and see me with such dirty paws. How lovely to see you, darling. Go and wash them this second. Who is your friend? Do sit down, Mr Er— There is nowhere, I'm afraid, in this part of the building, where I can encourage you to wash *your* hands.'

'I'm afraid,' began Nigel.

Jenny scurried away, in manner as in appearance no older than the scandalised girls in the upstairs dormitory. She giggled as she went along well-remembered passages to the dim cream paint of a well-remembered bathroom. She loved contradictory people. Sandro, who pretended aristocratic languor and was a dynamo. Colly, who pretended torpor and was a terrier. And Winnie, who pretended to be meek and shockable and was an unshockable latent *Mafiosa*.

She scrubbed her hands, sniffing the well-remembered smell of wholesome school soap. She found a gap-toothed comb and combed her hair.

When she got back to Winnie's room Nigel was refusing cocoa.

'What about that girl who disappeared?' she asked abruptly.

Miss Winstanley's face became wooden.

'It's important, Winnie. The one who ran away and nobody could find her.'

'There was,' Miss Winstanley said carefully, 'some two or three months ago, a child who very ungratefully deserted from our little community here.'

'Charlotte something.'

'Caroline Harper-Clarke. Her parents were quite abusive.'

'Could she have been kidnapped?'

'Her parents, as far as I know, never received any note from anyone. Any ransom demand.'

'Where and how was she found?'

'She never was,' said Miss Winstanley heavily. 'I have stopped brooding about it as often as I used.'

'There must have been quite a teeny hue and cry?'

'Yes and no. Yes, I know Sir George Harper-Clarke spent a great deal of money. At the same time they were terrified of publicity.'

'Publicity is how you find missing persons. Little blurry snap in the *News of the World*. Then when someone goes to a strip-club and on dances the birdie . . . '

'Of *course,* darling, as I *told* them. But no, it all had to be discreet. Sir George is Chairman of a number of companies, Lady Harper-Clarke frequently appears on the social page of *The Times* . . . '

'Oh dear.'

'So lots of private detectives came and asked impertinent questions – odious little men in macintoshes, costing I believe the *earth.*'

'Was she a nice girl?'

'Difficult. Not *evil*. Self-willed, over-indulged, an only child.'

'Beastly for her parents.'

'Difficult people. Her mother had been a beauty, oh, I *well* remember . . . '

'So Caroline is pretty?'

'Far too pretty. Old for her age. Dreadfully spoilt.'

'Bad habits?'

'I don't think I understand you.'

'Do you think she ever tried taking drugs?'

'*Quite inconceivable*. She was not a degenerate.'

'Why do you say "was", Winnie?'

'Whatever became of the child, Jennifer, it would be foolish to assume that she is continuing her education or living according to the principles by which we govern our lives here at Wapshott.'

'Would anybody have her measurements?'

'The sewing-room maids might have kept them. Whatever for? Besides, Caroline was still growing.'

'Why really did she do a bunk?'

Miss Winstanley shrugged. 'She was bored and restless. Girls nowadays mature so fast . . . I sometimes wonder if we get through to some of them at all. We seem *irrelevant* to them. Caroline . . . Caroline, I think, simply felt it was time she started to live.'

'Yes. Poor little beast.'

'Jennifer – what is your concern in this dreadful affair? How is Mr Heywood involved?'

Jenny glanced at Nigel before she answered. 'Another girl we know has just disappeared. Kidnapped. I slightly feel, some weeny instinct tells me, there might be a link.'

'You were always, Jennifer,' said Miss Winstanley drily, 'more inclined to rely on instinct than on the academic and intellectual disciplines.'

'Horribly true. I used to *bleed* for you all.'

'What do you think happened to Caroline?'

'I think girls of a certain type, meeting some *bizarrely* precise specification, are being popped into bottles and used for something.'

'White slaving,' said Miss Winstanley instantly.

'Yes of course, Winnie. But I think there must be more to it. The *trouble* they take.'

'Can I help?'

'Yes. Now and later. Later I'm not sure how, but I'm *groping* towards a scheme—'

'Oh Lord,' groaned Nigel softly.

'I bleed for you too, pet.' Jenny turned back to her old history mistress. 'What you can do now is somehow smuggle us out of here.'

'Out past whom? The Head?'

'Yes, there's no need to worry Miss Trimingham. But also out past some gentlemen in the woodlands.'

'Who followed you here?'

'In a sense.'

'Right.' Miss Winstanley addressed herself, without visible surprise or shock, to the immediate problem. 'You offer no difficulty, darling. You can join a group of girls on a run.'

'In bloomers? *Heavens* what camouflage.'

'As to Mr Heywood . . . ' Miss Winstanley frowned. 'He would *not* be convincing dressed up as a mistress.'

Jenny gurgled with laughter. 'Then a master? Music-master? Like Figaro?'

'Yes. A thick scarf. A bicycle. A music-case. A pair of my spectacles.'

'I won't do it!' said Nigel.

'You wouldn't be happy here, love.' Then Jenny remembered the vibrating redhead. 'Or perhaps too happy.'

'It is not to be contemplated,' said Miss Winstanley primly.

'Couldn't we wait until it's dark?' pleaded Nigel.

'I'm not *wild* about their finding our car.'

'Oh.'

Jenny's appearance, among a mauve-legged party of girls thought to need exercise, did not excite much surprise. Old girls who visited the school often, nostalgically, joined in at netball or hymn-singing.

The party was formed up in a back passage by a strap-pig young games-mistress who had been non-committally briefed by Miss Winstanley. They ran, in a close-packed group, out of the back, past the bicycle-sheds, and down the drive. Jenny, anonymous in borrowed bloomers, kept between a sixteen-year-old called Daphne on her left and Samantha, slightly older, on her right. Daphne's enormous bust jounced up and down as she ran. Samantha's cheeks crimsoned like Canadian apples.

Jenny was vividly aware of hard, imagined eyes looking out from the dense rhododendrons. She kept her own eyes to the front and tried to run with the wobbly self-consciousness of a teenager.

At the foot of the drive she peeled off from the party and ran warily, just off the road, to the hidden M.G.B.

She got into the car, lit a cigarette, and sat waiting for Nigel.

Nigel's disguise was a little more trouble but not much. Miss Winstanley conducted him downstairs; he was saluted, without suspicion, by an elderly mistress and a nice little matron.

At a side-door he clambered on to an elderly bicycle (it belonged to the night-watchman). Miss Winstanley said goodbye and wished him luck.

He pursued a snipe-like course over the gravel sweep in front of the house. The bicycle's steering was odd. Then he grew more confident and bicycled briskly down the drive.

He passed close to a tangle of laurel. A stick was thrust out, into the spokes of his front wheel. The bicycle toppled forward and sideways and Nigel fell over the handlebars on to his head. A blaze of fire filled his brain and he was out cold.

'Bring him round,' said a large dark man. 'He can take us to the girl.'

7

Nigel was conscious of a shocking pain in his head, the only reality in a world muffled in dark blankets.

Other sensations gradually forced themselves on him. His wrists hurt. His arms were pulled painfully backwards. His forehead felt wet.

A voice came from a great distance: 'Where's the girl?'

Nigel moaned and opened his eyes. He seemed to be sitting down, his back to a tree. His wrists were tied together behind the tree. His legs were untidily stretched out in front of him. He felt a flicker of childish annoyance to see how torn and dirty his trousers were. Expensive trousers. Probably no use to him at all, ever again.

His brain was clearing.

'Where's the girl?'

A big dark man stood over him. Beside him was a man with a depressed, respectable face, who wore a woolly muffler much like the one Miss Winstanley had lent Nigel.

Nigel recognised the woolly-muffler man. He had seen him in a pub off Berkeley Square. He had seen him hail a cab and then hurry off into the fog.

'Where's the girl?'

Did Woolly-muffler recognise Nigel? He showed no sign of doing so. He stared at the stiff black trees with a look of distaste.

'Where's the girl?'

Big dark man. Tamara had been examined by a big dark man. Nicola had been examined (prodded and defiled) by this big dark man.

Nigel was very frightened.

Nothing in his padded middle-class background prepared him for anything like this. For the use of violence and terror as a casual, a normal business technique. People of Jenny's background were brought up to a kind of savagery. They shot birds with guns and stags with rifles; they cheered as foxes were torn to pieces by hounds. There was blood on their hands from birth. There was no blood on Nigel's hands. He was a creature of well-lit streets and warm rooms and bright offices.

Nigel felt sick with fright, but his wits had fully returned.

'I shall get impatient soon, Sunny Jim.'

'In the house. In the school,' said Nigel.

His mouth tasted dry and dark brown. His words rattled painfully in his throat.

'Why?'

'She . . . I don't know. She likes it there.'

'Try harder.'

Nigel thought furiously. These people must be aware by now that Jenny knew about Caroline.

'She had some idea about a girl who disappeared.'

'What idea?'

'I don't know. I just drove her here. I don't know what this is all about. She smashed up her own car, she wanted a lift.'

Woolly-muffler murmured to the big man. The big man grunted at him angrily. He turned back to Nigel.

'Keep trying, Sunny Jim. Where's your car?'

'In a garage in Shaftesbury. The handbrake seized. We came here in a taxi. We came up through the woods. I was bicycling back to get the car.'

'The girl. How long is she planning to stay?'

'I don't know.'

'Guess.'

'I can't.'

'Okay, we'll come back to that. Seen any good slippers lately?'

'Slippers?'

'Don't make me cross. I want to know what happened to the slipper you found. I want to know who's been told about it. I want to know very soon.'

'I don't know,' said Nigel wildly. 'I don't know anything about any slippers.'

'Maybe,' said Woolly-muffler glumly, 'it wasn't him. We never properly saw the bloke.'

'And in the pub?'

'I didn't properly look. I couldn't say.'

'Let's find out.'

Woolly-muffler nodded. He seemed to know what finding out involved. Nigel had a sick feeling that something horrible was just about to happen to him.

Woolly-muffler lit a cigarette. The big man took it with a look of distaste. He took hold of the waistband of Nigel's trousers and with a sudden heave of great violence he pulled them down to Nigel's knees. Nigel's underpants and white thighs looked pathetic and vulnerable.

They were vulnerable. The big man burnt Nigel in the thigh with the cigarette, at the same time covering his mouth with an enormous hand. Nigel screamed with pain, screamed uselessly against the big hard hand over his mouth. The unbearable jab of agony made him forget his head and wrists. He nearly fainted again. The pain seemed the more shocking because it was so close to his unprotected masculinity.

The big man let go of his face and he whimpered. He knew that he was not being brave.

'Let's talk about slippers.'

Nigel drew a shuddering breath. 'I'd tell you if I knew. Don't do that again. I don't know anything.'

'We'll see. Keep trying. How long is the girl staying in that school?'

'She said – she said as long as she had to. Until she got a message to come away.'

'Message who from?'

'I don't know. The police.'

The big man handed the cigarette back to Woolly-muffler.

'Filthy habit. I may want it again.'

Woolly-muffler puffed at it morosely. He seemed to enjoy it neither more nor less after the use to which it had been put.

The rhododendrons pressed round them, dark and impenetrable. In spite of the horrible pain of his burnt thigh Nigel was aware of his head and of his wrists, and of the discomfort of the hard uneven ground.

'Till she gets a message. Do you think if we sent her one of your balls in an envelope she might come out quicker?'

'I don't know,' muttered Nigel.

The shiny-faced Sergeant now pushed through the thick bushes, with an attempt at stealth.

He glanced down incuriously at Nigel. Then he said to the big man: 'Another lot coming out. Three old bags and a few girls.'

'Okay. Stay here and look after Beautiful.'

The big man tied a scarf (Miss Winstanley's scarf) suffocatingly tight round Nigel's mouth, then walked quickly away. Woolly-muffler followed him. Shiny-face grinned at Nigel without humour and began to whistle softly and tunelessly.

Nigel tried to vomit. The gag stopped him. He panted and heaved.

Visions of knives and of axes, of cut-throat razors and of garden shears jumped giddily into his mind.

Shiny-face put his hands in his pockets and looked at the treetops.

Two long, white bare legs flickered between leaves. There was a small crunch of leaves or twigs. Shiny-face half-turned, but by then he had been coshed. His knees buckled and he fell in a tidy tweedy pile.

'Poor love,' murmured Jenny. 'Keep still.'

His gag was off.

'Get away,' he whispered harshly. 'It's you they want.'

'Keep still.'

There was a scraping noise. His hands were free.

'Upsidaisy,' said Jenny. 'No time to waste.'

Nigel struggled to his feet, with Jenny's help. His head swam and pounded. His trousers fell to his ankles.

'I haven't any either,' said Jenny, still in schoolgirl bloomers. She looked extraordinarily sexy. 'Pick them up and off we go.'

Nigel held his split and ruined trousers up to his waist with his right hand; his left arm was round Jenny's shoulders. They shambled, like incompetents in a three-legged race, into the woods and away.

'I waited for what seemed like a year,' said Jenny, who was driving. 'And I just didn't dare take on two of them. Poor leg.'

'You saw that?'

'Quite put me off smoking.'

'I was a coward.'

'No, love. Very far from it. Nobody could have done better. Unlike me. My awful unforgivable error was assuming there were only the four in the Jaguar. How rude Sandro will be when I tell him.'

'Will you tell him?'

'Yes. Hum-hum. I wonder, will they think I'm still inside the school, after you've left your teeny tree-stump? Or think we had somebody with us? What will they think we'll do?'

'What will we do?'

'Whatever Sandro says. I'll stop and ring him up in a minute. We both need a drink.'

'Dressed like this?'

'Oh dear.'

Sandro solved things with great speed.

He brought (in a car of which there was no other example in Great Britain and only three in its native Italy) some clothes for Nigel, ludicrously too large, clothes for Jenny, which were needless, and her air ticket. Her passport she had. He had managed to put her on an immediate flight, and arranged for her to be met at Turin. He also brought dressings for Nigel's broken head and the burn on his thigh.

'I will ring you up at Montebianco when I have decided what is to be done,' said Sandro.

'Actually, darling, I think I've already decided.'

'Yes?'

'So obvious.'

'I know. It may be the only way. But I will try and think of something . . . less exciting.'

'*Do,* pet. See you soon.'

She kissed Sandro and Nigel on the right cheek of each, and disappeared swinging her suitcase. She looked like a nice but silly girl of seventeen going on a holiday to play lots of tennis and read Mazo de la Roche.

'Not one word of any of this must be said to anyone at all,' Sandro said to Nigel in the bar at London Airport.

'How do you know what Jenny is planning?'

'As she said. It is obvious. It is, perhaps, the only idea. It will take some preparation. I hope we shall not all soon die. I understand you are in love with the mad girl whom they kept the other night?'

'Not mad,' said Nigel hotly.

'I see it is so. Love,' sighed Sandro, 'what energy it wastes. You will wish to help, then. Also the grotesque Miss Winstanley.'

'Can she help?'

'She is basic to the plan which I am hoping to replace.'

'Did Jenny take her gun to Italy?' asked Nigel.

'No,' said Sandro seriously. 'A cosh only. If she needs guns there are many. Do you want a gun?'

'Do I need one?' asked Nigel, feeling that things had got beyond his control.

'Not yet, I think.'

Jenny was met by Sandro's chauffeur and whisked in the Iso Griffo to the foothills of the Alps.

They got to Montebianco at ten.

She had eaten on the aircraft, but Memo the butler and Consolata the housekeeper insisted she must be hungry. She sat alone, at ten-thirty, under a chandelier of Venitian glass the size of a grand piano, at one end of a table at which she had seen thirty-six people sit. Memo, in white gloves and livery, stood behind her chair. She ate *prosciutto,* trout, and fruit, but could not be induced to tackle *lasagne* or *scallopina di vitello.* Memo was displeased by this abstinence. He put it down to illness.

She slept in one of the principal spare bedrooms on the second floor. The bed was enormous and ornate. The contents of a well-stocked bar and a delicatessen were arranged on a bedside table: Sandro's own grappa, Scotch whisky, brandy, mineral water, biscuits, salami, a bowl of fruit. The pictures made Jenny shudder: a St Sebastian whose plump, greyish-white tummy was bristling with arrows like a pincushion; another saint on a griddle, being barbecued by pagans in fifteenth-century hats; a crucifixion by an Umbrian primitive with a diseased imagination.

The morning was soft and misty, with a feeling of hidden but imminent growth. Jenny greeted the rest of the indoor servants, then the mechanics, the gardeners, the secretaries. She killed an hour with the English magazines stacked in Sandro's study – a room of wood and leather, a parody of a St James's Street club. On the wall were photographs of big game and racehorses, and two small Guardis. There were shelves of poetry, of Rowland Ward's big game records, of sailing books, and of books about guns and drugs and crime.

At eleven Jenny had a Campari and soda and went for a walk in steep woods behind the castello.

The world was dripping and mysterious. It was very quiet.

It was the lull before the storm.

8

'Much as I miss the little rosebud, and much as I wish we had her along,' said Colly to Sandro on the V.C.10, 'I can't help feeling glad that Jenny's in purdah for a spell.'

'I also,' said Sandro. 'Wrapped up in cottonseed.'

'In *what?*'

'In cotton-wool.'

They came back to New York, and Colly made inquiries. They flew to Miami, and drove to Fort Lauderdale and a little beyond. They found Matt Warren in the saloon of his yacht.

Matt Warren was drinking Bloody Marys. He seemed to have crawled into the little world of the yacht like an animal which has been hurt and badly frightened.

They had learned more about Matt Warren in New York. He was Board Chairman of Ferrando Metals. Like the Fords, but unlike most active American industrialists, he had inherited a substantial slice of the company's equity. He was therefore very powerful as well as very rich.

He was surprised to see Colly, but cautiously hospitable. He remembered him, of course. It was difficult to forget someone with a reputation for almost incredible torpor.

He was introduced to Sandro, of whom he had heard as owner of some notable Italian pictures.

Sandro was interested in the yacht. The yacht was for sale.

Like Colly himself, Matt Warren was known as a passionate and lifelong sailing man.

But the yacht was for sale.

'Why?' said Colly.

They had decided, on the flight down, that nothing was to be gained by pussyfooting around the subject. This egocentric tycoon was not going to spill the whole dreadful story (if there was one) to one comparative and one total stranger suffering from mild curiosity.

'Don't get the time for it,' said Matt Warren.

'Let me try something on you, Mr Warren,' said Colly. 'If we're completely off the beam throw us out and we'll apologise as we hit the jetty.'

'What the hell are you talking about?'

'An upper-class seventeen-year-old English girl called Caroline Harper-Clarke.'

A sick spasm crossed Matt Warren's face. Sandro, watching him closely, knew that they were right.

They talked for three hours. They heard about the white ketch, name unknown, with a crew of two, in the Caribbean. They heard about a film. They heard about three payments, enormous even by Matt Warren's standards, huge and elaborately discreet, over the past month.

They came up on deck. They looked across the shining water at the Brighampton Yacht Club clubhouse. Big hardwood trees came down almost to the water each side of the neat marina. There were a dozen yachts tied up, one as small as thirty-five feet, one nearly two hundred. Others were anchored. Colly told Sandro that several members of the club sailed regularly in the Caribbean. All of them were rich. Many of them got very drunk occasionally, especially on vacation from their important and exhausting jobs (if they had any jobs), and especially in the tropics, and especially on board yachts, where ordinary rules of conduct apply only intermittently and with reduced force.

'You see, Mr Warren,' said Colly, 'this formula they have could get to be a regular industry. It has to be stopped. You have to go to the cops.'

'And face a manslaughter rap?'

'Tell them not quite everything,' said Sandro gently.

'Yeah . . . '

Two days later Colly and Sandro were back in New York. Colly homed, by arrangement, on the quiet tedium of the Vander-huysen Club.

He sank into a leather chair in the backgammon room, where conversation was permitted. He stretched out his long legs as though he had had a hard morning.

He was brought a gin and tonic by Fred, the Scottish barman; he read a *Yachtsman* newly arrived from England.

At twelve-thirty he was joined by Matt Warren, who sank down and stretched out his legs exactly as Colly had done. He really had had a hard morning.

'I've been with the cops,' he said softly to Colly. He signalled to Fred, then sighed. 'Told them part of the story.'

'So now what?'

'I wait till I get instructions for the next pay-off. Then I tell the cops and they work out some kind of an ambush.'

'We'll be there.'

'How will you be there?'

'We know some cops.'

Matt Warren frowned. 'Is this the kind of thing you spend your time doing?'

'I spend my time fooling around yachts. Sandro spends his time fooling around girls and pictures and race-tracks.'

'But—'

'Matt, we're in each other's confidence. Keep it that way?'

'I guess so. Jesus, yes.'

In a dark bar near Grand Central a man in a black turtleneck was softly playing the piano. A bar curved round the piano. Late-night people sat on stools and listened to his smooth modern piano and talked quietly.

There were a few tables. Two girls who still had faint hopes of profit sat at one; adulterous couples at two others; Matt Warren, Sandro and Colly Tucker at another.

'Personal and Confidential on the envelope,' said Matt, 'and mailed to the New York office. One typed sheet inside.'

'Same as before?'

'No. Different every time.'

'Typewriter?' asked Sandro.

'I.B.M. Electric.'

'Traceable?'

'The cops are working on it.'

'So,' said Colly, 'what's the scenario?'

'I drive in my own car to a place called Rillington Beach.'

'Sounds like Long Island.'

'No. New Jersey coast. A little shantytown establishment – you get a cabin for a quarter, a boat for a dollar.'

'How do you know about it?'

'Jersey police. It's at the end of a three-mile dirt road off the highway, and the cops figure they'll drop in a car behind me to make sure I'm not being tailed.'

"That is right,' said Sandro. 'I would do so.'

'A place like that,' said Colly, 'these people can get away by land or sea.'

'Or air,' said Sandro. 'Helicopter. They have money.'

'They do,' said Matt Warren.

'Goddam full-scale military operation,' said Colly. 'Army, Navy, Air Force.'

'I'm scared sick,' said Matt Warren.

'So would I be,' said Sandro. 'It is foolish to feel brave.'

'It's late to be lonely,' said a girl in a fur coat at the next table.

'Then off you go and do something about it,' said Colly amiably.

'Your mother must be proud of you,' she said nastily.

Sandro grinned at her, then made a noise like a bear. Colly waved at a waiter.

The pay-off was to be in three days' time.

The police helicopter waited in a little clearing in the dense woods of this useless part of the New Jersey coast. There was a lieutenant in a heavy tank-coat, three uniformed officers and the pilot. They had rifles, pistols, submachine-guns, grenades, smoke and tear-gas.

'Ten minutes,' said Colly to the Lieutenant.

The Lieutenant nodded, his expression mixing respect with resentment. Mr Tucker, it seemed, was a friend of the Commissioner, and a generous contributor to police orphans' funds. He was writing a book.

And this Count was some kind of foreign hot-shot, a V.I.P., a visiting fireman. The top brass ladled the butter on to guys like this, but they got in the way of the men down the line.

Not that either one of these rubbernecks could do any harm today. The thing was sewn up.

Another helicopter was berthed further inland, ready to cover the exit from the dirt road into the highway.

There was a squad of police on foot, well hidden, at a carefully chosen ambush-point on the dirt road.

There were road-blocks ready on the highway (but hidden now) in each direction.

There was no way of watching the sea from the sea. There was no fishing hereabouts; nobody took yachts out at this time of year; any vessel anchored or hove-to or even circling would have alerted the blackmailers. Colly's helicopter had to cover a sea-borne get-away. But the engine would not be started until the getaway had begun, or Matt Warren and maybe others would be killed. Helicopters make a lot of noise.

It had been possible to insert only five cops into the beach buildings and area. They had to be hidden where the gang would not go, which eliminated the comfortable office. The beach-huts were folded up and stacked during the winter. So a boathouse held two men, well hidden but with poor visibility. Under the jetty, in a frogman suit, waited a third. If they came or went by boat he could do something to the boat, with a harpoon-gun with an explosive tip, or with wire mesh to loop over the screws, or with a neat little limpet-mine. The fourth cop was in the upper branches of a pine tree at the edge of the woods; he had a good field of fire except immediately below him, but like the rest he was primarily an observer. The fifth was buried; they had scooped a foxhole in the shelter of the stacked sides of the beach-huts, camouflaged it thoroughly, and armed it with a bipod-mounted medium-calibre machine-gun.

None of these men except the swimmer had any line of retreat. If they fired they gave away their positions.

All five were in radio contact with the helicopters, the ambush party, the road-blocks, and the mobile headquarters. The waveband had been selected at random by computer; it was to be changed at irregular, predetermined intervals.

Matt Warren's Cadillac was reported eight miles from the dirt-road intersection, travelling at 38 m.p.h. No tail was visible.

'There's something a little wrong in all of this,' said Colly to the Lieutenant.

'Yeah?'

'If I wanted to walk into a trap, this is where I'd choose.'

'We let them in, we get them bottled.'

'If we can see that, so can they. And they picked the place.'

'From their point of view it's perfect, Mr Tucker,' said the Lieutenant patiently. He wanted to be mentioned favourably in the book this jerk was writing. 'This season, it's off the edge of the world.'

'But like you say, when they're in they're bottled.'

'They don't know we're here with a cork. Listen. Warren had the guts to come to us with the whole story.'

Three-quarters of the story, thought Colly.

'Like how many guys in his position?' said the Lieutenant. 'Most of them pay and keep paying, or run, or take a jump from a high window. Listen. Remember that suicide, two-three months back, an oil man with yachts and every goddam thing you can name? We smelled something there and the boys really dug. Spread that guy's whole life out on a clean table and shone bright lights on it. *Nothing.* Listen. That man was actually *happy.* So we figure he was being blackmailed for one little episode, maybe way back, one time he went wrong, one thing he was really ashamed of. A dame, a little boy, a hit-and-run, some little fraud way back, could be anything.'

'You say this man had a yacht?'

'Every goddam thing you can name. Warren's the smart one. But I'm telling *you* it must have taken guts to come and tell the truth, in a stuffy office in Police Headquarters, with a shorthand writer and six-seven guys standing around.'

'That's true,' said Colly.

'A courageous guy. Added to which the risk, Mr Tucker, Jesus. The danger he's in, here today.'

'But he's the goose that lays the golden egg.'

'No sir. You can't go on blackmailing a man who's already spelled out the whole story to the cops.'

You can this time, thought Colly.

A wind from the sea set the tall pines creaking. The sky was steel-grey.

In these woods you would never expect to hear bird-song.

The radio crackled. Matt Warren was five miles from the intersection. He had slowed to thirty. There was other traffic on the highway. No tail was identified.

The officer in the pine tree was called Harvey Snell. He was frightened but happy.

In his farm boyhood – a life dominated by potatoes and tractor-oil – he had devoured the crime comics (preferring The Phantom and Doctor Fate) and the pulp-magazine stories about gangsters and cops. Westerns left him cold. The others could have the war. He lived in a dream-world of prowl-cars and the Homicide Squad.

On a fine day, across the flat untidy New Jersey farmland,

you could see the shining towers of Manhattan.

'Captain Snell, Homicide . . . ' The sirens would wail as the wheels screamed on the wet streets.

When he joined the Force, and did well in the written tests, and became a medal-winning rifle shot, his mother had been scared but his father said his prayers and was resigned.

Today was Harvey's first time on an operation like this. The youngest man in this hand-picked detail. The one they put up into the pine tree. The front-line eyes of the whole State Force.

His tiny radio bleeped. Warren's Caddy was two miles from the intersection, travelling at twenty-six.

Harvey Snell had once brought his girl to this beach. Myrna. She had married, in the event, the son of a motel manager from Newark – a sharp dresser, a man with shady friends. Maybe she was happy; Harvey thought not. Either way, he well remembered the day when she had still been his girl. Three hundred people on the beach. Peanuts, popcorn, beer, ice-cream sodas and sundaes. Cars had honked up one a minute all day. The sea was dotted with heads and with canoes and little sailboats. There were lifeguards with beautiful tans. A fat young Jewish housewife gave Harvey the eye. A good day. The high spot of that romance.

Today the place could hardly look more different. Metallic sky. Lead-grey sea sullenly rustling over the shingle. The beach-huts, the tatty umbrellas, the Coke booth, the peanut stand folded away till summer. Sand blew across the concrete and the boardwalks. Someone had left a small, stained flag on a flagpole; it tugged and fluttered, a sad little vestige of summer. Harvey guessed that the man who was supposed to pull it down found the pulleys rusted and thought: the hell with it, a fifty-cent flag. Loudspeakers yawned to all four points of the compass from a pole by the clapboard office. Harvey remembered the Hit Parade numbers of the moment blaring from those gaping mouths, that nice summer day with his girl. They decided one of the songs was 'their song'. Harvey remembered the song without pain. He hummed it, excited at the prospect of action, keyed up, a little scared.

Bleep. A Mercury wagon with a trailer had turned off the highway on to the dirt road.

Harvey shifted in his little cocoon of camouflaged canvas. He had binoculars, rifle, earphone, neck microphone. He knew that, to anyone unsuspicious of his particular tree at his particular height, he was virtually invisible.

Crackle from the helicopter's radio. The Mercury had just passed the detail on the dirt road. The trailer seemed to be some kind of tank, with tubing and stopcocks. Four men in the car, none identifiable.

'First beetle in the bottle,' said the Lieutenant to Colly with solemn joy.

Beetle. Bottle. These two words, falling into the suffocating excitement of waiting in these drab pinewoods – these silly words spun Colly's mind back to the Fall of the year before last. A year and a half ago. Colly in Scotland to stalk red deer in a world of heather and stinging rain, of cold grouse eaten in your fingers on an unprotected hillside, of gigantic late dinners in the shooting-lodge with kind, slow-spoken men with famous names, men who could climb all day and who sunburned easily. Of terror, coming up like a Gaelic ghost from the mist-filled glen, bringing death and extortion. Of his hand being taken and his life saved by a clear-voiced, idiot-talking girl with a baby face and beautiful legs. Of her friend summoned from somewhere, dropping out of the sky, ugly and middle-aged and pretending laziness, and of the three of them fighting across Scotland and becoming eternal friends.

Colly's life was transformed from the Fall. His public face of sybaritic idleness had never thereafter showed one crack to the world, which lost him respect, and some friends and at least one important girl.

Crackle. 'Warren has just turned off the highway. Speed

around eighteen.'

Matt Warren, alone, scared, with an awful lot of used bills in airline bags on the back seat of his car.

Matt Warren, who . . . an English girl, thought Colly. And Nicola would be another. And so it would go on. Until they stopped it. And maybe today they were stopping it, when all the beetles were in this massive bottle.

Bleep. A black Oldsmobile had turned on to the highway from the secondary road to the Campbelltown oil refinery. Four men. Heading for the dirt-road intersection.

As expected.

Bleep. On the dirt road a minute and a half behind Warren.

Hell, thought Sergeant Carl Hands, the immobile frogman under the rickety jetty. Two cars, no boat. No chance to use the new harpoon with the explosive spearhead, its charge throwing forward to make a small hole on impact and a big mess beyond. No chance for his flexible steel mesh, plastic-coated to hide shine and muffle noise. No satisfying bang from his limpet-mine. No fun.

Sergeant Hands shifted a little. He wriggled a flipper to drive away a cramp in his instep. He had been here a long time. He was bored.

Bleep. The Mercury wagon was nearing the beach.

Harvey Snell was the first of the party to see the Mercury, from the dark branches of his pine tree. His eyes widened. The radio had said 'trailer', but this was a trailer he would never have expected. A trailer right out of his boyhood, a farmyard familiar. Harvey's Dad had one like it – same make, even, Harvey thought – which bounced along behind the Dodge truck or the IH tractor. It ran off the tractor engine. It was a tank with a pump. You squirted fungicide at the fruit-trees with it, insecticide at the potatoes, selective weedkiller over the grazing land. You could fool around with the jets – the coarser the spray, the smaller the pattern, the longer the carry: or a fine spray over a big area, keeping the vehicle moving.

What could these boys want with an old farm sprayer?

The wagon stopped. Four men got out.

Yes, the right men. All masked.

Three fiddled around with the sprayer, linking the drive by a flexible cable to the car's crankshaft, uncoiling hose, bolting on the nozzle. One of the gang, Harvey thought, knew what to do. The other two fumbled. They got on quite fast, just the same. The fourth man stood by, watchful, with one of the army's newest submachine-guns.

Harvey noted the number of the wagon (routine; someone up the road would surely have taken it too) and the make of the spray equipment, which quite likely nobody else would know.

He softly reported the masks, the gun and the preparation of the sprayer into his neck-mike.

'*Spray?*' said the Lieutenant. 'Insecticide and weedkiller? Has Snell gone crazy on me?'

'Something here is wrong,' said Colly again.

Sandro had prowled away. He prowled back again. Hearing Colly, he nodded. These people were rolling cheerfully into a trap. They had some way out of the trap. It was likely to be violent and effective.

Harvey Snell saw a Cadillac bounce expensively from the dirt road out into the open. The man with the gun flagged it down. It stopped near the office and Matt Warren got stiffly out. The man with the gun kept him covered while one of the others left the sprayer and came over to the Cadillac. He unloaded dozens of little bags – Pan Am and American Airlines, Braniff and B.O.A.C. and United and Eastern, Air France, Alitalia, Lufthansa, K.L.M. He checked the numbers and the contents. He nodded to the man with the gun, who said something to Warren. Warren slowly turned round, his hands up. He was hit once, not very hard, with a small club.

The gunman continued to watch; the other man, to Harvey Snell's amazement, began to arrange the airline bags into gay little rows. Three rows, the bags divided equally into three. Red, green, blue, smart little bags with zips, permitted on the overhead racks of aircraft cabins, redolent of paperback books and nightgowns, of aspirins and duty-free cigarettes.

Harvey reported this nursery game being played, like building-blocks, on the bleak grey beach. A man with more imagination might have pictured the expressions on the broad, hard faces of the Lieutenant, the Chief, all the men in the woods and the helicopters.

It seemed the sprayer was ready to go.

Spray what? Spray why?

One of the men went to the back of the wagon and opened the double gate. He drew out three pipes.

Harvey Snell blinked. He reported the pipes.

Dull grey metal pipes, Harvey said, steel or aluminium. Each about seven feet long.

Something to do with the sprayer?

No. Two men, between them, threaded a pipe through the handles of each multi-coloured row of airline bags.

So they had a lot of bags strung on pipes. To carry, sure. To *carry,* when they had two *cars*? Three cars?

The third car, the Olds, bumped out of the woods over to the office. Four men got out, all masked. One glanced at Warren, checked the sprayer, checked the airline bags and the pipes. The others seemed to be reporting progress; he seemed to be the boss. Harvey could not see his face or observe any meaningful mannerisms. He was dressed like all the others, in a neat coat and a dark grey hat. A small hat. He had a small head. Except for the masks, they might all be commuters who travelled daily to an insurance office.

The boss took a slow, comprehensive look round. He indicated the door of the office. Another man immediately kicked this to pieces. The two of them went in. A light went on inside. They had found the master-switch, then. The light went off. Then the four big square loudspeakers wheeped and crackled.

'ANYBODY WITHIN EARSHOT WILL NOW COME OUT, SLOWLY, WITH ARMS RAISED.'

Four more submachine-guns had appeared from the Mercury. They were swung casually all round the perimeter of the beach area,

'I REPEAT, ANYBODY WITHIN EARSHOT WILL NOW COME OUT, SLOWLY, WITH ARMS RAISED.'

Harvey Snell remembered the brazen note of these loudspeakers. 'Their song', his and Myrna's, that hot day, that high-spot day. Or the nasal Jersey City voice of the manager calling in boats which had stayed out over the hour the people had paid for.

'I DO NOT WANT VIOLENCE. YOU WILL NOT BE HARMED IF YOU COME OUT NOW, SLOWLY, WITH ARMS RAISED.'

The men in the flimsy boathouse heard it. They glanced at each other, grinned and fingered their guns.

The man in the foxhole heard it. His flat, pale-blue Teutonic eyes crinkled with contempt at the corners; he stroked the breech of his machine-gun.

Sergeant Carl Hands heard it, up to his neck in the dirty grey sea, in the weed-grown darkness under the jetty.

'I WILL NOW COUNT TO TWENTY. YOU WILL COME OUT, SLOWLY, WITH ARMS RAISED, BEFORE I REACH TWENTY. ONE TWO THREE FOUR FIVE—'

They heard it clearly in the helicopter, rasping over the trees. 'We're not going to need this thing,' one of the uniformed men had just said.

'SIX SEVEN EIGHT NINE TEN—'

The rest heard it on their radios, syncopated as it came to them from microphones at different distances from the loudspeakers.

'ELEVEN TWELVE THIRTEEN FOURTEEN FIFTEEN—'

Three of the men dropped their guns and went to the sprayer. Another started the engine of the Mercury wagon. Spray. A fine mist, first, over the beach buildings, the boathouse and the stacked canvas. Then more power. A jet at the trees, soaking them, crashing between the twigs and fronds and soaking the ranks of trees behind.

Harvey Snell sniffed.

Gasoline.

He was suddenly sick with fear because he knew what was going to happen. He tried to speak into his mike but he gagged over the words.

At full stretch the spray arched over the near trees and smashed down on to the tops of the scrubby trees behind.

They swung it methodically, left and right, up and down. A long arc of grey liquid quartered the surrounding woods.

It thudded momentarily on to the helicopter's thin metal skin. 'Rain?'

'SIXTEEN   SEVENTEEN   EIGHTEEN   NINETEEN TWENTY. OKAY.'

The two men ran out of the clapboard office. The arch of the jet faltered, then abruptly died. Empty. A rustle of newspapers, a flare, something thrown.

And then a picture of hell, of a city under an H-bomb.

A great sheet of flame tore over the beach buildings and almost immediately another rose like a window-shade, vertically, up the dark front of the woods.

The man in the foxhole, burning, tightened his fingers on his trigger, in too much pain to know what he was doing. Bullets sprayed up into the air as he fainted. The gun thudded on, harmlessly, until the magazine was empty. The gunner was dead before the gun stopped firing.

The men in the boathouse screamed and struggled to their feet. No gasoline had touched them, but it had sprayed the walls and roof. They struggled out through incandescent flame. They made beautiful targets as they were silhouetted against the flame. They were shot.

Harvey Snell was a torch in a tree which was a torch. He was still alive when his branch broke and fell, but he was dead after he hit the ground.

The screaming of all four was audible over the appalling noise of fire on the radios of the rest, until the transmitters were burned. It gave the party in the helicopter a fractional warning. Colly, by the door, was out first. He turned to help.

'Run!' shouted the Lieutenant to Colly, but turned himself to help his men.

The enormous horror of the fire walked through the gasoline-soaked trees and fell on to the helicopter like the hand of a god.

Colly, Sandro, the Lieutenant and two others were out.

They backed away from the blaze. They heard the screams of the others. There was nothing they could do.

'Gas-tank,' said one of the cops.

'Ammunition,' said the Lieutenant.

They turned and ran.

The woods were dry now. The clearing had been the ultimate of the sprayer's range.

A boom behind them was the helicopter's gas-tank. Other

explosions followed – the sharp, ragged cracks of small-arms ammunition, the big thuds of grenades. They lay flat, hugging the dry pine-needles. A piece of metal zinged close overhead – the base-plate of a grenade, or a part of the helicopter's engine. 'On, out of this,' shouted the Lieutenant. No gasoline now, but miles of bone-dry pinewood. They had to run and keep running. They were out of radio contact. There was a quarter-mile of inferno between them and the gang, if the gang were making a move.

The gang were. Eight figures set off demurely along the beach. Plenty of room, and the wind was blowing inland. Three pairs of men held the seven-foot pipes, one at each end. As they strode along the smooth shingle the little bags rocked and swung. The other two men had guns and watched front and rear. There was no need to watch the flank.

The Fire Department checked the blaze at the highway.

The second police helicopter made it to the beach. Matt Warren was dead: asphyxiated. He was no longer a goose with any golden eggs to lay. Sergeant Hands was in shock.

The gang was presumably picked up either by car or by boat, either up or down the coast. None of the men had been clearly seen or could be described. Except that one had a small head.

The Mercury and the Oldsmobile had both been stolen in New York City. The sprayer had been stolen from a nearby farm. The I.B.M. typewriter used for Matt's instructions had been stolen from a motel on Long Island; it was recovered in a scrap-metal dump; it yielded no fingerprints. Twenty-two feet of steel pipe, one-inch gauge, might have been stolen from a builder's yard in a suburb of Jersey City. Their stock-keeping was bad: a clerk was fired. It was impossible to determine where the load of gasoline came from.

The investigation came up against a complete blank wall.

Colly and Sandro started back to London.

'I had one small hope,' said Sandro in the aircraft, 'that we could catch the boss and destroy this thing.'

'Goddam boss was there, it seems. Keeps a very personal eye on everything. A meticulous guy, as well as being fussy about girls.'

'The boss was there,' agreed Sandro. 'And then he was not there, having lit his little barbecue. We are stupid, you know that? We of all people should expect these bonfires.'

'Still we keep getting surprised,' said Colly.

'Surprised when violence is so large and shocking. Surprised that successful criminals go to such lengths. That is where we are stupid. With this man we must be no more surprised.'

'We have to surprise him, I guess,' said Colly wearily.

'Yes. It must be Jenny's plan. There is no other plan.'

'I know it. I don't like any part of it.'

'Nor I,' said Sandro glumly. 'I am very, very frightened.'

9

'We know what they're doing and why,' said Colly presently. 'But not who or how.'

'There is also some why which is puzzling still.'

'Jesus, Sandro, the why has never been a puzzle. Warren's contribution alone . . . '

'But, *caro,* the girls. The fussiness. The trouble. The complexity. Why?'

'I keep trying to figure out a different way of attacking this whole thing.'

'I also. There is none. We must do this. Or more men will go to ruin and more girls will go to hell.'

'I have a horrible feeling little Nicola Bland is there already.'

If she was she didn't know it.

She lay, under deep sedation, on a dirty sheet on a dirty table in a dirty room. She was naked. Her pulse was very slow; her breasts hardly moved when she breathed.

A man in a dirty white smock was mixing something glutinous in a bowl. A single naked bulb cast a harsh white light on Nicola's damp and pallid body. A transistor radio emitted, at moderate volume, the sound of a fuzzy beat-group; between numbers, and over the hearty voice of the disc-jockey, could be heard the cries of coloured children playing in the street.

The man in the smock stirred his mixture to the beat of the music on his radio.

A greyish bubble appeared at the corner of Nicola's half-open mouth. The man popped it delicately with his finger. He stroked and fingered her body. A fat black fly buzzed interminably round the light-bulb.

A precocious, babbling, naughty, vulnerable, very upper-class schoolgirl with long fair hair laughed at the surprise on the face of an elderly schoolmistress.

She said she was called Phyllida Pearce.

'And we've got to be quick,' she said, 'so please, Winnie, don't be surprised at anything.'

'Very well, Jennifer,' said Miss Olivia Winstanley. 'But it does seem to me that they might recognise you.'

'No, Winnie. You hardly did and you've known me for years. Poor Nigel just simply didn't, for a minute, and he's known me for three years.'

'But, Jennifer dearest—'

'And they've hardly seen me. Whizzing along in a car in the dark, that's all. Never close to.'

'Photographs?'

'In a tiara, in *The Queen,* laughing like a hyena at a joke about hunting.'

'They recognised you when you came out of that dreadful restaurant of yours.'

'That was circumstantial, Winnie, don't you see? Predictable. They were confidently expecting a particular girl to come out of a particular door. My face didn't come into it.'

'I shall be thankful, Jennifer,' said Miss Olivia Winstanley with pursed lips, 'when all this is over.'

'Yes,' said Jenny. 'Me too.'

Between three members of the little group in the National Gallery and the fourth there was a noticeable difference.

The three were none of them ugly or retarded girls – they were merely normal girls. Their minds no doubt ran from time to time on boys, and sex, and guilty matters; they had normally erotic dreams and day-dreams; they had smoked cautious cigarettes and drunk wine in their fathers' houses. One was skinny; two carried a good deal of puppy fat; the faces of all three seemed to have a long way to go before they achieved adult complexions or contours.

The fourth was unmistakably a handful: a knock-out, a degenerate. You could guess she was the only child of indulgent and badly-behaved parents, probably both many times married. You could assume that her juicy prettiness had attracted a variety of premature sexual advances, few rejected. You could sense experiments with pills and funny cigarettes.

Nobody much noticed the three normal young ladies or their elderly schoolmistress – London is full of such parties as the school holidays begin. A lot of people noticed the fourth child. A policeman licked his lips. An art-gallery attendant sighed with lust. A Cypriot waiter contrived an obscene caress while removing a bowl of moussaka. She was that sort of girl.

With iron self-discipline Jenny restrained herself from looking for any of the people she had seen or who had been described to her by Nigel and Tamara. There were no such people. She was a very silly sixteen-year-old riding for a fall.

There could be no let-up: eyes might be everywhere. She giggled when the waiter's forearm covertly stroked her breast; she pouted sexily at her reflection in the Ladies at Burlington House; she lagged behind the others in public places, and when she looked about her it was with wide, avid eyes that wanted something but didn't know what they wanted.

Nothing happened for four days.

Nothing might happen for forty days, or four hundred. The eyes, whether blinking over a woolly muffler or some quite different pair, might be searching in Brighton or Bedfordshire, in Berkeley Square where Nicola had been spotted, or in Hampstead or Huntingdon.

But there was no other way of going about this.

And Soho seemed the most likely.

Nothing happened for four days. They were trying days. The Soho district would not normally have attracted a culture-hungry little group of this sort. But the old schoolmistress had – she loudly and frequently said that she had – a taste for and knowledge of foreign cooking. Archaeological trips to Greece and the Dordogne, cultural pilgrimages to Florence and Rome, had converted her (she explained to anyone who would listen) from roast beef and two veg to subtler and spicier foods. Believing as she did (and as she often said she did) in a full education and a well-rounded personality, she introduced her charges to one or two little restaurants which London friends had recommended.

Which was why the group was to be seen in Sink Street after lunch on a sunny Friday.

They had been bowed out of La P'tite Auberge (Dmitri Kuprassos, proprietor). They passed a bookshop full to bursting with magazines full to bursting with breasts and buttocks. The naughty fourth girl lingered. They passed the door of Stripsville – 10 Lovelies 10 – which was adorned with photographs of some of the lovelies. Music belched out of the door which gave immediately on to a flight of seedy stairs; a wall-eyed young man in a kind of leather cardigan leant in the door waiting for suckers. The naughty fourth girl lingered and the young man offered her a job. She giggled, glanced at the photographs appraisingly and strolled on. She knew that she had more sex appeal than all the ten lovelies staked out side by side on a velvety lawn at midnight.

'What's a nice girl like you,' wheezed a soft voice, 'doing in a street like this?'

Woolly-muffler. Sad and respectable. We're off.

'I'm with my friends,' said the girl in her high, clear, arrogant, upper-class schoolgirl's voice.

'You can meet friends, be a lot more fun than them.'

Of course the child should have hurried on. But she fractionally lingered; she showed a trace of indecisiveness.

'Yers, kiddie. You slip away and come with me to my little club where I go. Ooh, very respectable, more of a social gathering. There's actors and dancers, gangsters—'

'Gangsters?' said the baby, her wide eyes widening.

'Large as life. I can point them out to you.'

'How terrifying,' drawled the deplorable girl, not looking terrified.

'Not arf,' grinned the woolly-muffler man.

She said it was entirely out of the question. Because she didn't dare? No, because she couldn't. Rows enough already. Schoolmistress stuck like glue and could make life hell.

'Perfect—hell,' said the girl in her high young voice.

Well, if she found she *could* slip away, say between eight and ten, here was how she got there and here was the name to ask for. All cosy she'd find it, lovely new friends, see a bit of life, have a drink or two, dance if she wanted—'

'With a gangster?'

The man laughed, a noise like steam being pushed through straw. 'With a murderer if you want.'

'High time too,' said Jenny.

'Oh dear,' said Miss Olivia Winstanley. 'I do hope and pray and trust . . . '

The club was called Jack's and it was pretty dull. It looked like a pub which nobody had taken any trouble about. There were tables and rickety chairs and a jukebox. A man in a fancy-knit pullover (possibly Jack) stood behind a bar. The customers were polite. The men were mostly dark and wore dark suits; some of them had ties, though these were not normally pulled up fully to the collar. The women were off-duty prostitutes, or the girl friends of the men, or both. It was very brightly lit. There was a fruit machine which made nearly as much noise as the jukebox. Many of the men were whispering to each other, but when they called greetings they were loud and jolly.

Jenny came down the stairs in the clothes Phyllida Pearce would have selected for such an occasion. A respectable coat (because she had no other); expensive shoes (because she had no others); a red mini-skirt and a baby-blue see-through blouse with a black bra delightfully visible beneath it. Her long fair hair was draggled and she wore white lipstick and heavy eye make-up.

She looked like a sixteen-year-old lady dressed up as an eighteen-year-old tart trying to be a twenty-year-old lady.

A scarred Jamaican smelling of Marijuana intercepted her on the stairs.

'Is Mr Andy Fergusson in the club?' asked Jenny regally, as though asking for an uncle at the Cavalry Club.

'How old are you?'

'Thirty-five.'

The Jamaican laughed in an unnerving soprano, and led her down and into the club-room.

There were three of them at the table. Her friend Woolly-muffler, now without his muffler; a big dark man; and the Salisbury police sergeant with the very shiny face.

There was quite a long way to walk over to their table, under the glare of the strip-lighting, across the tartan linoleum on which no one was dancing.

Men looked up. They nudged each other. Every man in the room looked at this nutty mystery wiggling across to Ginger and his mates. What a bird. Dirty old cradle-snatchers! Her big little tits in that black brassiere, her arse swinging like a bleeding pendulum. Two bleeding pendulums. Every man in the room except Percy the Peel (who worked in a strip-club in a long blond wig, and had fair old tits himself) could have used a half-hour in the back of a Zodiac with this one.

Jenny was frightened, crossing the linoleum dance-floor under the pitiless lights.

Woolly-muffler was the eyes. He might or might not also be

a knife-thrower.

The big dark man reeked of extortion and protection. He might be robbery with violence, but he looked more like a puller of fingernails and drawer of teeth with rusty pliers in dirty back rooms. He had stripped Tamara and Nicola. He had burnt Nigel Heywood. He had visible authority. He probably ran the English end.

Jenny had been positive, talking to Winnie, that she would not be recognised. More positive than she felt.

It would be disagreeable to be recognised.

She sat down and the big man patted her on the shoulder.

'Glad you could make it, dear. Did you tell the old lady where you were coming?'

'Good *gracious* no. Can you *picture* what she'd do?'

The three men beamed. Woolly-muffler wheezed and nodded. Shiny-face asked her what she would have and went heartily over to the bar to get it.

Big dark offered her a short fat cigarette. It was made of funny paper. As soon as Jenny lit it she got the sweet, aromatic, sickly, not disagreeable reek of pot. Not strong: mixed with tobacco.

Big dark's eyes were on her as she inhaled. An important moment; she must start right.

'Divine man,' she said in her high, precise voice. 'How beady to know this was just what I wanted.'

'Ever sat too long in one place, dear, an' got pins and needles?'

She looked at him with wide blue eyes which had no expression but plenty of understanding. 'So difficult to come by needles. I never seem to meet the right people.'

'Now you have.'

'Then we might try knitting.'

This saucy repartee bit was chancey. But they had kept Nicola and dropped Tamara back into the river. They had kept Caroline Harper-Clarke, by all accounts a pert and confident damsel. Anyway, they laughed now. They repeated the joke to Shiny-face when he came back from the bar with drinks, and he laughed boisterously.

He had been terribly convincing as a police sergeant. Perhaps he had once been one. Did he shave every hour on the hour?

Jenny accepted her vodka and bitter-lemon and sipped it. She tasted the drug immediately. (She could tell a St-Emilion from a Medoc, blindfold, when they were nine months old and undrinkable.)

They were looking at her. She sipped again. The sweet heavy smoke of her cigarette hung over the table.

She thought the drug was sedative rather than knock-out. 'It is only possible to act drunk convincingly after a little drink,' Sandro had once taught her; it was only possible to act doped convincingly after a little dope.

So she giggled, and looked round the room with curious, hungry, contemptuous eyes, and drank.

The jukebox was fed by a big blonde in purple satin, who then began to dance in a joggy old-fashioned style with a tiny man with a pencil moustache. Two girls, long-ignored by their busily whispering escorts, got up to jitterbug morosely. One was chalk-white with straight black hair, the other coffee-brown with a cloud of pink hair.

'Sharmy,' said Jenny loudly.

She meant to say 'charming' and say it dopily. She said it more dopily than she meant.

A lot of cigars were being smoked. The air grew thick.

The music of the jukebox pounded into Jenny's head, seeming to come in by one ear and not go out by the other, but stay inside, packing her skull tighter and tighter with electronic twangs and booms.

She carefully planned a Phyllida Pearce remark: 'The jukebox is—loud.' She opened her full, white, wet sexy lips. Nothing came out except a little high moan.

Pleased with the effect she moaned again, and then giggled.

It seemed to her that the table was ridiculously large. The big dark man was now a tiny dark man, shrunk by great distance.

He seemed to be talking, but he was too far away to hear.

She knocked over her drink, still two-thirds full. It soaked her left knee and dribbled stickily down her calf. She was aware of this and dabbed at it pettishly with her sleeve.

Shrugging seemed to be going on. Lots of people shrugged at each other. She felt her arms taken, and she was lifted to her feet.

'Sorry, Jack,' someone called one inch from her ear.

The music pounded. Clang-whizz went the fruit machine. Concentric circles throbbed outwards, as though somebody had dropped a stone into her liquified brain.

'What a waste.'

'Enough is sufficient.'

'Four bobs' worth.'

All the men in the room watched Ginger and his mates help the silly bitch out. Probably been drinking all afternoon. Probably been mixing drinks and pills. Smell that? There you are then. Oh, I don't mind *pushing* it but I wouldn't *touch* it. I caught my bleeding nipper, wham, I don't mind telling you. No end to it once you start.

'Who is Ginger, Jack?'

'No idea.'

'No wish to be nosey. You know me.'

'Frien' of a frien' of a frien'. West Country, maybe? Three Scotch it is and thanking *you*. Don't know his mates neither.'

'Nor the bird neither?'

'Nobody won't know *her* much longer. Spilt it everywhere.'

'Upsidaisy,' said Jenny with sudden clarity.

They emerged on to the street – Anderson Street, Soho North, still strewn with the squalid flotsam of its market.

They were in a car. Her wet left leg was cold.

'Okay, Roddy.'

They drove and then walked and she was helped down some steps and into a room with a bright light. The light hurt her eyes.

'Strip.'

She whimpered and plucked at her belt.

'Okay, Murch.'

They stripped her. She stood, rocking, not resisting. Her skin crawled with horror. When she was naked she giggled and said: 'Nice?'

The dark man inspected the skin of her arms.

Pity no pin-pricks, thought Jenny muzzily. Her brain was very slowly and uncomfortably working again. Nicola must have had some, so Nigel fibbed. Caroline probably had some too, so Winnie fibbed. That might dish everything. The hell with bloody loyalty.

The dark man was still looking at her, frowning. She wondered insanely what to do – how to persuade him she was the next one for the purpose, convince him she was degenerate enough.

She was not keen on standing naked in this cold, bare, dirty room with the dark man frowning at her as though she were a suspect Argentine beef-carcase.

Shiny-face lit a cigarette. The angle of his head and of his cheek-bone made him suddenly recognisable. He was Ginger-whiskers shaven. And transformed by his shave, because the whiskers were what you had noticed. Very effective. He had grown his bristles for one public act, whipped them off for another, and but for a mnemonic accident the link was invisible.

Someone in this, thought Jenny, knows what it's all about. Someone cleverer than these nasty people. Perhaps with a tiny head.

The big dark man's face was completely expressionless. The others waited.

Surely, thought Jenny. Surely I'll do.

She moved her body slightly, oscillating her hips, rubbing her thighs together, flexing her pectoral muscles. It was not much; it was a very great deal.

She felt utterly shoddy and despoiled.

'Nice?' she said in a little greedy voice, sounding far dopier than she was.

'Quite nice, thank you, Lady Jennifer Norrington. You wanted it and now you've got it. And I hope you enjoy it, but I don't think you will.'

10

Nigel Heywood disliked the clothes in which Sandro had dressed him and the job he had been told to do.

He was a pansy.

It would have been difficult to say why this was so obvious. But the other men in the saloon bar of the Irish Bagpipes in Anderson Street either shrugged slightly to each other or else smiled at him decorously. He was just another one, a stranger from somewhere, managing as best he could. No one would interfere with him or give him a second thought.

He was clearly waiting for somebody. He glanced at his watch, and frowned and clucked, and fiddled with an evening paper, and drank bitter lemon. Whenever anyone came into the bar he looked up eagerly. He waited for a long time.

He was by the window and he could see the little yellow door from which, in the street, muffled jukebox music could be heard.

A tarty and very young girl came clip-clop down Anderson Street. Nigel thought she reminded him obscurely of someone he knew. With a shock, and only because he expected her, and even then only because he had been told what she would be wearing, he recognised Jenny.

His disguise slipped a bit. Something tense and angry showed through the gentle, careful, self-effacing mask. He was not a marvellous actor. But no one noticed.

Everything now depended on the kidnappers using the front door when they came out.

There was a crawling interval. The Irish Bagpipes was like any other pub in any other back-street, only quieter. Even the regulars greeted each other softly. Faint music hummed from a speaker; glasses tinkled; talk was muted and confidential.

They did use the front door, and Nigel was galvanised.

Two men in dark clothes, supporting between them a pathetically stumbling little tart; a third man, drably respectable, trotting behind.

Nigel sidled out of the saloon bar after a final frowning glance at his watch. Only two men noticed him go: one middle-aged, with a crapulous face and a white turtleneck, one younger, with a yellow silk scarf. They smiled and shrugged to each other: 'Good luck to him.'

Sandro, driving, could not directly tail people who were walking. At least not people as alert and professional as these. Nigel could, innocently strolling wide-eyed through wicked Soho. And Sandro could follow him. The white trousers would be visible a long way away.

The party from Jack's turned left down Anderson Street. Nigel followed, well behind. They crossed the road and turned right down an alley. Nigel paused at the corner, looking about him, evidently lost.

A beat-up Anglia belonging to the Puncinello Mediterranean Fruit Co. chugged to a halt close behind him. There was a muffled altercation between the driver and a well-wrapped elderly woman beside him. Soho wops, always waving at each other. Probably arguing about the best way to get home, or having a blood-row about the year great-uncle Giuseppe bit the greengrocer.

Nigel glanced down the alley. A Vauxhall's doors were open and its engine ticking over. He turned, scratched his head, and strolled to the fruit-van.

'Black Vauxhall Velox, IBB 623, any second now.'

'Can they go the other way?'

'No room to turn.'

'*Capito. Grazie.*'

The big black Italian from the Puncinello Company pointed directions to the stranger. The stranger nodded, thanked him and walked off towards Leicester Square.

The Vauxhall rolled out into Anderson Street and turned north. The van followed – one of thousands like it in every part of London.

Nothing strange or suspicious had happened – nothing at all.

The Vauxhall kept to ill-lit streets; it buzzed along demurely, never exceeding thirty.

'I thought tailing was difficult,' said Miss Olivia Winstanley.

'Usually, yes. But they could not be expecting us. No one could imagine anyone doing what Jenny is doing.'

The Vauxhall drew up at last in a short street called Lamancha Place, near the Kentish Town tube station. The fruit-van chugged by. Two men got out of the Vauxhall's back seat with a sad, shambling creature between them. A third got out of the front passenger seat. The car immediately drove on. All this Miss Winstanley had time to see before the fruit-van rounded the next corner. She also saw the number of the house. Sandro saw that many houses and flats in the street were to let, and that it was a coloured street.

The Vauxhall went on and the noise of its engine faded and vanished. Sandro nodded to Miss Winstanley and she got out, hauling after her a cardboard suitcase with a rope round it.

'I am sorry,' Sandro murmured. 'Almost certainly nothing will happen tonight. Perhaps for days nothing. But—'

'But we dare not leave Number 17 unobserved. Don't worry about me, Count.'

'I think I need not. Tomorrow early we will make a superior arrangement.'

In Lamancha Place that night an elderly Frenchwoman with only a little English knocked helplessly at several doors. She was looking for her nephew. She had an illegible address scrawled on a piece of paper. She was greeted with politeness, some ribaldry, no surprise. There was no room for her in any of the houses which were occupied; they were bung full. The unoccupied places were locked. Some Grenadans tried talking to her in French, but she could not understand their debased slaves' argot, nor they her Parisian.

White teeth flashed in black faces. There were cooking smells, and other smells, and nostalgic steel-band records, and other music, and London Transport uniforms, and great numbers of children. There was much goodwill. No one had heard of the nephew Marcel. The old woman remained tenaciously convinced that this was the right street; she pottered up and down it until the small hours – until the last radio was finally switched off and the crowded little colony slept. She did not knock at the door of Number 17, even though lights continued to show through cracks in its curtains after the rest of the street was dark.

Colly had been a reserve tail behind the fruit-van. A blinking brake-light told him that all was under control. He sighed with relief – a superficial flicker of relief on top of his deep and nagging worry about Jenny. He went home to the Connaught and to bed.

He was annoyed to be woken almost immediately by Sandro on the telephone. But he nodded and mumbled agreement, and arranged a call for eight o'clock, which surprised the night porter, who was used to Mr Tucker's morning indolence.

At four-thirty the old woman in Lamancha Place apparently gave up hope; she shambled southwards, and was never seen in those parts again.

Just before she reached this decision, a travel-stained Bedford truck had pulled up in the street. The driver needed a sleep. He was a big dark foreigner. He lay back in his cab, breathing gustily. His face was in deep shadow. He was near Number 17, on the other side. He was one of six drivers using the street as a lay-by.

The minute after their office opened in the morning, a firm of back-street estate agents undertook to show an unfurnished flat to Mr Edmund Barrow, newly arrived from Kingston but with money to spend.

Mr Barrow had the mixture, not unknown in Jamaica, of light eyes and European features with a dark coffee skin. Some slave-owner of great genetic prepotency had left him this useless legacy, just as others have implanted red hair and blue eyes and a pale skin on features of an entirely negroid cast.

A Trinidad Indian took Mr Barrow to several streets near the Kentish Town tube station (it seemed that good communications were important to this client) which were either too expensive, or too narrow and noisy, or in one case – otherwise ideal – contained a cousin of whom Edmund Barrow was frightened.

At last they came to Lamancha Place, at ten o'clock in the morning, and Edmund Barrow paid a deposit for the first floor flat in Number 16. He also consented to buy, at an inflated price, the greasy fragments of carpets and curtains.

Quite soon afterwards a small van drew up with Edmund Barrow's possessions. A few chairs, a camp bed, and one large cabin-trunk. This was extremely heavy, and caused swearing. The door shut behind the new tenant.

The commotion of the moving-in evidently woke the driver of the Bedford truck. He yawned and spat and started his engine and the Bedford ground away towards Central London.

Colly undid the great birds'-nest of knots in the ropes round his cabin-trunk. He opened it and Nigel Heywood got stiffly out and stretched.

'Keep right away from the window, boy. I'll watch for now.'

'I hope the radio's all right after that bump.'

'I hope you are.'

'I'm fine. Bloody cold.'

'Plug in the electric kettle. Let's play house,' said Colly. He did not move from the crack in the curtain.

The flat was bitterly cold. A small electric fire warmed only a yard of air directly in front of it. Colly's feet and hands were soon numb. He never took his eyes off Number 17, the anonymous basement, the station to God knew where.

Nigel said: 'Do you think Nicola is there too?'

'Was, I guess.'

'Coffee?'

'Thanks.'

'But of course,' went on Colly gently, 'if your kid is already on her travels—'

'We can only find her by following Jenny.'

'And maybe not then. I'm sorry, but you have to face it.'

'And maybe not then,' repeated Nigel thickly.

They took turns by the window, turns huddled by the little fire. Colly dressed up again as Edmund Barrow, making himself look at once cocky and ingratiating, and went shopping parsimoniously in the little groceries and butchers of the area. Later he produced a savoury mush which warmed Nigel's middle but could not reach his fingers and toes.

They smoked cigarettes. Neither suggested a drink.

From 11.35 a.m. they were in occasional radio contact with Sandro. They spoke French (Sandro's fluent and strongly accented) in the very unlikely event of their messages being accidentally monitored by the enemy.

Night. Nigel's fingers were so cold he could only write with difficulty. The flex of the little electric fire was stretched to its fullest extent. It was still some feet away from him: it might have been a mile. He flexed his fingers painfully, looked at his watch, and made another entry in his log of events in the house opposite.

This, after eleven hours, recorded nothing of any interest or value. The big dark man and the 'Sergeant' had left and returned and left again. Though heavily outnumbered they were not the only whites in the street. They were not conspicuous. They looked completely boring. It was possible to feel that this was a ridiculous charade, this sitting in the bitter cold and endless peering across the street at a gritty facade with curtained and uncommunicative windows. Except that Jenny must be inside there, in squalor and extreme danger; except that the big dark man who looked like a butcher or a bookie had burnt Nigel's thigh with a cigarette; except that the same dark man and his boss had taken Nicola.

Nicola was 38,000 feet above the Atlantic, but she didn't know it.

For Jenny semi-consciousness succeeded unconsciousness, and then consciousness slowly and painfully succeeded semi-consciousness. But there was not much difference between the three.

The hands again. Blearily, helplessly, Jenny associated the hands with the squeak of bedsprings and with a woolly muffler.

The hands once again exploring her body. Pinching, groping, caressing, squeezing, fingering.

Jenny was just awake enough to want to scream with revulsion. She was not awake enough to do it.

Firm footsteps in a passage.

The hands disappeared. The bed creaked as weight left it. Blankets over her body.

Hands gripped her arm. The jab of a hypodermic.

Waves of grey-green sleep, falling, blackness, oblivion.

The owner of Vauxhall IBB 623 was covertly identified and indignantly approached. Sandro fulminated about the buckled wing on his beloved little Fiat.

The owner condoled. He himself had been breathalysed six months before, on the way home to Bromley after an office piss-up at the Cumberland. He'd tried to sell the car, but the best offer was one-twenty. Which he thought a bleeding insult. So he'd lent it on a semi-permanent basis to a friend. Fellow called Roddy. Not rightly sure of his surname. Well, more of an acquaintance, yes. No idea where he lives, where he operates. Scrap-dealer, junk, antiques, something like that. Oh yes, we'll get it back after I've done my year. Sorry you had trouble, doesn't sound like old Roddy. Of course the bastards will whip your no-claim bonus, won't they? If things are the same with you as they are here.

Yes, of course, if I see him I'll tell him.

The car's owner was getting a fiver a month for the Vauxhall. There was no need to shout about that. It came in readies, very nice. This was all he knew and all he wanted to know.

Things were quiet in Lamancha Place.

On Sunday the dark man came and went twice. On Monday the 'Sergeant' came and went once, bringing groceries (it was to be assumed) in untidy parcels. Obviously the others, whoever they were, never went out. Too sensitive? Too busy?

Colly felt ill imagining what they did when they were busy: what Jenny was being subjected to.

On Tuesday, on Wednesday and on Thursday nothing happened at all. The light was on all the time, in the little room by the basement steps. Nothing else.

'That house has no back,' said Sandro on the short-wave radio. 'I have looked most carefully. There is no way they could get her out except by the front. So if you two are both quite truthful *she must be there.*'

They waited and watched. The time crawled.

Towards evening on Friday Colly saw the Trinidad Indian estate agent leading a big and boisterous black family to

Number 17. He unlocked the door. They poured in. Handshaking and jubilation went on. Noise began, music and the shouting of children.

Colly, dark and cocky and ingratiating, a Jamaican with sharp Aryan features, scuttled out of his own dismal little flat and joined the almost-party going on outside and inside Number 17.

'New neighbours?' he said to the estate agent.

'Ah, Mr Barrow.'

'What became of those white men? Red-faced feller?'

'They were off beginning of the week, four-five days. Paid up, moved away. Didn't like the area, maybe.'

'Leaving anything behind?'

'Haha! Need anything? They left one bed, one ol' table. These people are glad of those things.'

'Otherwise,' said Colly, 'this place been completely empty?'

'What you expec', man? Golden coins?'

Sandro sat with his head in his hands. Nigel stared blindly out of the window. Colly paced up and down like a madman.

'Oh God,' cried Sandro. 'They have made fools of us utterly. And Jenny has vanished to—ah, where?'

11

Sandro felt the bitterness of defeat. The agony of knowing that he had betrayed someone who trusted him, and whom he loved.

They had been so clever, and they had been routed. They had been devious, subtle, foolproof, and they had been set watching an empty mousehole, empty for a week.

And the mice were ravening animals.

And Jenny was in their power, in the power of people who burnt policemen to death and drove men to suicide and sacrificed girls like matchsticks, like cigarette-ends.

And they must know who she was.

Sandro railed at himself: 'I said how difficult it was to tail a car in traffic, but how easy it was because this time we were so clever. It was easy because they made it easy. They waited for me at every corner. They led us to an empty house and left us watching it. They came and went a little, and we nodded and said cleverly: "Yes, this is right." Fool and cretin and murderer,' Sandro muttered to himself, *what have we done?*

'How did they get her out?' croaked Nigel.

'Obviously she never went in. As soon as we went round the corner they put her on the floor of the car and drove off. It was easy for them, because they knew about us, and they knew we did not know that they knew. Because we were idiots and assassins . . . '

'I was there,' said Colly, 'I could have followed them.'

'*I know*. And we never thought.'

'You think,' said Nigel, 'you think they're both out of the

132

country?'

'I guess.'

'Then we must search the whole Caribbean.'

'Christ, boy,' said Colly, 'yeah, but that's hundreds of islands, thousands of yachts, a million goddam square miles of sea. And how do we know the Caribbean? Why not plant the girl and the camera in a motel in Los Angeles?'

'No,' said Sandro, controlling himself. 'For many reasons. A yacht is perfect for them. No maids, no snoopers. Also no Mann Act. Also it is mobile. You can take it to the sucker. Also your three suicides had all been recently to the Bahamas, the Virgins or Jamaica. Also people repeat in patterns, you know?'

'Sold,' said Colly reluctantly. 'Now tell me how you search for one small girl in one large ocean.'

'Two girls!'

'Sorry, Nigel. You're perfectly right. Two.'

'I will tell you how,' said Sandro.

In the ludicrously named 'garden flat' of a Council block near the Battersea Power Station, a man from the Board of Trade inspected an amusing statue.

It was quite a respectable piece of nonsense.

It was a full-sized Negress, done in plaster and painted. The head was swathed in a lurid turban, the torso naked, the hips and legs draped in more bright folds of 'fabric'. To an untrained eye it had quite an eighteenth-century look. The anatomy (what could be seen) was accurate, the finish a little crude. It lay in a lidless crate on a table.

'Once again I congratulate you,' said the man from the Board of Trade.

The man with the woolly-muffler smiled. The man with the pasty face gave a deprecating shrug.

'It's not a forgery, see. We're not pretending it's old.'

'All the same I'd almost call it a work of art. Honestly I would, I'm being quite sincere. I wouldn't mind her myself, standing in the hall, lovely. Though *what* the wife would say . . .

'Aha, well, the Americans are kind about them,' said Pasty-face. 'Take all we can send. Which, my time not being my own—'

'How many does this make?' 'Only the three this winter. I really only call it a hobby, mind.'

'Profitable hobby.'

'That I don't deny.'

'Nice little dollar-earner,' said Woolly-muffler. 'Same like whisky and tweeds. The government ought to love us.'

The Board of Trade man laughed. He signed the appropriate forms and customs-clearance was now automatic.

'What does the American importer say about them?' he asked 'What date does *he* put on?'

'Aha. That's no concern of ours.'

'But in point of actual fact,' said Woolly-muffler, 'I b'lieve he's quite legit.'

'Why do you air-freight them? What's wrong with a ship?'

'Always ask ourselves,' said Pasty-face. 'Seems barmy. But you know what Americans are like. Want everything yesterday.'

'Also handling,' said Woolly-muffler. 'She's quite fragile. We wouldn't want her turned on her face, or a couple of Jaguar cars sitting on top.'

'And she's not more than two hundred pounds.'

'Another thing puzzles me,' said the Board of Trade man. 'Why's her eyes shut?'

Pasty-face shrugged. 'We goes by their drawings.'

'It's unusual. They generally have those great goggling eyes. The originals, I mean, the wood-carvings.'

'Ah, but like we said, we're not pretending she's genuine.'

'If Mister Rich in New York City wants her sleep-walking, then sleep-walking she is. It's easier to model this way, too. I don't know how we'd manage for eyelashes.'

Foam rubber and expanded polystyrene were packed round the statue, the top was screwed down, and official seals were pasted over the joints.

The thing was an amusing curiosity, practically valueless – a companion, no doubt, in some huge apartment, to ugly indoor plants and phoney paintings.

'She'll probably end up as a lamp, with a bleeding great hole in her head.'

All three men laughed.

'I will tell you how,' said Sandro. 'You have a lovely reputation, Colly *caro,* for being most idle and most rich. To these you will now add a reputation for being most drunk.'

'Oh Jesus.'

'And for all the time chasing girls in a most crude way, especially when drunk. You will make a lot of noise, and everyone will notice and talk. And presently an ear will pick up this noise and this talk, and then, perhaps one day a white ketch will come, and you will be asked to get drunk on the ketch.'

'It's a chance,' said Colly after a pause.

'Yes. No more.'

'Where will you be?'

'I think in attendance, quietly. By a radio. Nigel also.'

What?'

'They needed just one girl, but later another girl, yes? Why another girl? It must be another yacht, I think. We shall have to take both yachts. You will help. I expect not more than one of us will be killed.'

Nigel's mouth was dry. 'But my job.'

'Leave it.'

Nigel looked at Sandro blankly.

'I think you are better than that job. Jenny thinks also. And it is not sensible to worry about the future when there may be no future. It is quite plain what you must do.'

'Yes,' said Nigel. 'It is, isn't it?'

'You must be out of your mind,' said Nigel's boss.

'I don't think so.'

'Who's bribed you away?'

'No one.'

'If it's a few hundred a year more I suppose we can meet it.'

'It isn't. I'm not going to another company. I'm going abroad.'

'You must be out of your mind.'

Colly travelled separately. If by any tiny chance he were seen with Nigel by someone who knew Nigel then their plan, this new plan, was dead before it started.

He travelled alone. He was a very rich and very silly man looking for another yacht to buy. He mentioned this to friends in New York, where he paused on the way to collect clothes.

'God rot you,' said John Millet, 'you asked me to sail down with you in *Perelandra*."

'I did? Sorry as hell, John. Would have been a tiring trip.'

'Now if I want to go sail I have to charter something.'

'You do that.'

'Yeah, but with you it would have been free.'

'But tiring, boy, tiring.'

He flew Pan Am to Barbados, spent a luxurious night at Sam Lord's Castle, bathed in the crashing East Coast surf, then flew B.W.I.A. Viscount to Grenada. The taxi-ride over the mountains to St George's was as breathtaking as ever, and his driver ('my name is Joseph') was a well-briefed guide. Nutmeg and banana, coffee and cocoa and coconut leaned over the tortuous road. Old women mended the crumbling verges stone by little stone. In the villages children carried baskets and buckets on their heads, explaining the wonderful carriage of this tall and small-hipped people. Streams gushed from cliffs, and ferns and creepers with fat wet leaves sprouted out of the tumbled slabs of the hillsides. On top of the island the circular volcanic Grand Etang lake was as smooth and blue as a plate. All very different from the arid poverty of the dry islands, or the well-barbered agriculture of Barbados, or (God knew) the commercialised playgrounds of the Bahamas.

In St George's Colly hired a self-drive Morris 1100, and booked a room at the Cavendish, in the town. If he had to loaf, he preferred to loaf within spitting distance of the yacht-moorings; the somnolent pleasures of the Grand Anse Beach hotels were a different world – nice, but not this trip.

He went to the Kingfish Bar, and met some yacht-skippers and crews and sun-purpled charter-parties. He drove unsteadily to the Papaya-Papaya Nightclub and danced a Soul, to the polite derision of the local experts, with a Barclays D.C.O. secretary; she had a skin like café au lait silk and a body which seemed an exaggeration. He laughed and shouted and sweated. He made a fool of himself; but he made no enemies. A few people remembered him, of course; there was a feeling, a regretful feeling, that he was getting a little more ostentatious and a lot more drunken.

He spent the morning at the yacht company. Two yachts were thought to be for sale, one now out on charter. He inspected the other minutely, appearing to nurse a hangover. It was quite a good yacht. He hit his head on the boom when he came up on deck after looking at the auxiliary.

There were eight white ketches tied up at the jetties which more or less met Matt Warren's blurred description. Four of these were American, three English, one Canadian. There was no reason why any of them should be the scene of Matt's appalling evening out; there was equally no reason why one shouldn't. This racket was mobile. They did it to Matt in early February in the Virgins. They could pick up their other marks in Antigua, Martinique, Guadaloupe; or up in Peurto Rico or across in Jamaica; or they could go up to Nassau, maybe further up to Miami or Fort Lauderdale, maybe as far as Bermuda. Why not? And legitimate charters as a cover meantime. And a different skipper and crew meantime, quite possibly, so a description of George and Lyn (or whatever they were really called) would mean nothing to anybody.

Put yourself inside the mind of the opposition. Where would

you go? Christ, anywhere there might be a lecherous American with a lot of money. The Caribbean is a big sea. The Antilles is a lot of islands. George and Lyn could go wherever the fancy moved them. They would deliberately avoid a pattern.

Grenada was as good a bet as any. A thriving centre of yachts now they'd built the new slips and the chandlery. But the whole thing was sticking pins in maps. Colly had the sick feeling that he ought to be in Nassau or Montego, English Harbour or even Brighampton. All he could do was stay, and establish a loose and loose-lipped character, and hope for an invitation like Matt's: and meanwhile contrive to get a look at all white ketches.

One of the Americans was a motor-sailer; Colly felt sure that Matt would have so described her, even though to a landsman she might have fitted. The second had a crew of four and looked as though she needed it – an old yacht with a lot of heavy gear and hard work. She'd be a pig to take in or out with only two men, even under power. Most doubtful. The third and fourth answered pretty well. One was full of a party of Chicagoans who seemed reluctant to go to sea, in spite of the money they were paying; the owner-skipper was a middle-aged New Englander, the two crewmen local boys. The other was being refitted below by a local agent; the owner was expected shortly. Two of the English yachts answered. Their skippers were a little brown retired Colonel, a man like an athletic walnut: and a big gingery Scot who spoke with gloom about the future political stability of the ex-colonies. The third was an unpainted tub with a squalid saloon: wrong. Finally, the Canadian yacht fitted in all obvious particulars. The skipper was a charming Nova Scotian whom everyone knew; he was waiting for a party from Halifax, cousins of his own.

Nuts.

Four of the yachts that fitted had blue cushions in their saloons. All had shiny tables. Five had photographs of sailing-ships. None was ever available for bare-boat charter.

None ever went to sea except with her normal skipper and

crew.

Nuts.

The weather was firmly magnificent – wide blue skies and a stiff, reliable sailing-breeze. Colly's green eyes began to look very pale in his brown face. He borrowed dinghies from yachts and sailed them out into the long spectacular bay off Grand Anse. He capsized a fibre-glass Sunfish in front of the yachtsmen's bar; he was good-humoured about buying planters' punches all round. He became (or appeared to become) Homerically drunk on a day cruise to Carriacou.

He sweated up and down the steep eighteenth-century streets of St George's; he danced to steel bands and electric guitars; he spent money and chased girls.

It was necessary to make a wide-echoing reputation for wealth and for drink and for womanising, very quickly, before Nicola and Jenny dropped through their separate *oubliettes* into the same unthinkable hell.

Very quickly. Perhaps not quickly enough. It was not more than a chance.

A yellow-faced Englishman, long ago a doctor in Luton and still known as Doc, posted eleven airmail letters in the main Post Office in St George's. They were all addressed to Mr Henry Body, Yacht *Campanula,* care of the Port Authority; the addresses terminated with the names of eleven different islands.

The paragraph of typescript in each envelope was identical. It advised immediate arrival at St George's.

Doc looked in at the Cavendish bar on his way back from the Post Office, with the feeling of a good morning's work done. He had a pineapple daiquiri, sitting damply under the lazy fan of the bar.

He did not know Mr Henry Body, or the yacht *Campanula.* He did not know why Mr Body wanted news of rich Americans with time on their hands – except, at an obvious level, because charter yachts want customers. He did not know that he was one of a dozen layabouts and hotel receptionists and minor clerks, in various parts of the Caribbean, who kept Mr Body informed. He did not know; he did not want to know; he would have covered his ears and screamed if anyone had tried to tell him.

He only knew that he was paid a retainer of fifty Biwi dollars a month, a further fifty for each tip-off, and occasionally an unexplained bonus. It was really very little money. But of course it was very little work.

Mr Body, in English Harbour, opened his letter from Doc on the lawn outside the Admiral's Inn. He took a taxi to St John's, at the other end of Antigua. He walked delicately past the souvenir shops and the groceries and the Kensington Bar, and stepped delicately over the little rivers flowing down gutters which seemed also to be sewers. Friends in high places enabled him to use the short-wave radio in one of the airline offices; he urged his friends in Miami to send their niece down at once, saying that the sea air and the wonderful weather would do the kid a world of good.

A girl with dark hair, whose pupils were as small as pin-heads in spite of huge sunglasses, was immediately thereafter helped from a wheelchair into a Boeing. A fussy cousin sat beside her in the aircraft and the stewardesses were full of little extra attentions.

In the late afternoon they landed at St John's. Another wheelchair was trundled up. A taxi was called. The girl had very little baggage for an invalid. Soon after dark she was in the forward charter cabin of a white ketch called *Campanula*. At eight-thirty a man the others called Lyn gave her a jab with a meticulously sterilised hypodermic. Anyone could see she was in the best possible hands.

At first light *Campanula* chugged away from the crowded mooring. Out in the bay her sails were hoisted. She heeled to the trade-wind and headed south.

The convalescent girl was very pale and very pretty; she made very little sense. She was encouraged to sunbathe, not for too long, on the foredeck.

Mr Body stayed behind. He had business; he would join them later.

Colly woke up to find that another yacht had arrived, must have arrived during the night, threading the narrow passage dynamited out of the coral in the mouth of St George's harbour.

A day of exceptional heat and brilliance. Colly drove his 1100 round the waterfront to the yacht-basin, passing the Geest banana-boats and a tender from a cruise-ship full of docile elderly Americans. He sauntered down the wooden jetty, between the varnished masts of the close-packed yachts, threading the lazy morning bustle of washing, watering, victualling, all the busy bits and pieces that go with boats and which are tackled gently in the tropics.

Campanula.

A blond man with a deep tan was twirling a mop out of a porthole. A lovely dark-haired girl in a tiny bikini was sunbathing on the foredeck. The blond man was whistling, as expertly and as irritatingly as a professional *siffleur.*

Colly's antennae jangled.

He glanced at the yacht, which was a good-looking yacht. He ogled the girl for a moment. (He ogled every girl.) The girl seemed to be asleep. He sauntered on. He glanced at his watch, in the manner of a man who wonders if it is still too early for a drink.

He hoped they'd get on with their proposition quick.

They did.

Colly began his evening at five-thirty, in the Kingfish Bar. His first Scotch on the Rocks seemed to go down his throat in a twinkling. (It went, in fact, into the roots of the flamboyant tree at the edge of the Kingfish's dance-floor.) He took his second more gently. He even drank some of it.

'Ah – Mr Tucker, sir?'

'Yeah,' said Colly, looking up blearily.

A slim man with wavy dark hair looked down at him with shy good manners. He understood from talk around the harbour that Mr Tucker was in the market for a yacht.

'Yeah,' said Colly. 'Siddown. Have a drink.'

The slim man sat down and asked for a beer.

'My owners are thinking of selling, Mr Tucker, at the right price. Which I must admit to you freely I don't know what it is. They asked me to listen around for a possible buyer.'

'Being who?'

'Pardon me?'

'Your owners being who?'

'A syndicate in Miami. Hotel people, I guess. They practically never get away enough to use the yacht, what with their big season being *just exactly* the time when they'd like to get here if they could. Matter of fact we're waiting for *one* of them now, picking us up in a few days, *hopefully*. Plenty of time for you to see the yacht before he blows in, if the idea appeals to you, and then *maybe* you can talk business when he comes. I think that's what he'd like, Mr Tucker.'

'Sure. Tomorrow morning?'

'Be fine, Mr Tucker, just fine. And, uh, we're twiddling our *thumbs,* the four of us, be only too happy for an excuse to take her out.'

'Like to see her go, yeah.'

'She *goes,* Mr Tucker.'

'Nice lines.' Colly drank less of his Scotch than he seemed to be drinking. 'I'd like that.'

'I think,' said the slim man with a hint of archness, 'our lil cook saw you this morning.'

'Yeah?'

'And I'll bet you saw *her*. She's a great kid, Nikki. A real sport.'

The slim man winked. Colly winked back. He promised to come aboard the *Campanula* around ten.

Well, it was crude. Crude as hell, thought Colly. No less effective for that. The slim man was glib and convincing. The marvellous implied flattery of the girl noticing him was perfectly done. No surprise Matt had been suckered. There but for the grace of God, thought Colly, there but for the grace of God.

The two little fairies were competent, whatever you might think about them otherwise. The fenders were inboard and the hawsers coiled before *Campanula* had finished going astern to clear the yachts berthed each side of her. By the time they passed the cross at the mouth of the harbour the sails were up and drawing and the auxiliary was dead. Big headsail, main, mizzen, new and clean, with clean white nylon sheets and beautifully varnished blocks. This yacht was ship-shape, these people were seamen. Pity. Colly, stumbling, tried to help. George and Lyn needed no help.

'Take her, Mr Tucker?'

Colly nodded, and went aft to the wheel.

They pointed north up the coast, on a fine reach on the starboard tack. The wind was a little fitful because of the steep mountains behind the town. The yacht went beautifully, slicing the ice-green waves, heeling to port but stiff and reassuring, the three big sails in perfect aerofoil curves.

A schooner was motoring towards the harbour. Her sails were untidily furled and there seemed to be a lot of people on board.

'*Cressida*,' said George. He handed Colly an almost neat glass of rum.

'Where's lil cook?' said Colly.

'Why, getting lunch.'

Colly kept his eyes on the luff of the mainsail and on the compass. He treated the wheel rough, overcorrecting every small momentary change of course; he was steering confidently but clumsily, as though he was well-accustomed to yachts but in bad personal shape.

George gave him another drink. 'It's *party* day.'

They anchored shortly before one, in the lee of a dark-green cliff. There was no clatter from the galley, no sign of lunch in the big, shiny saloon.

'*Drinking* time.'

The girl appeared from below, gently propelled by Lyn. Lyn had changed into a minimal slip in a leopard skin pattern; he had a medal round his neck and a thin gold bracelet.

'Here's *Nikki,*'

Nikki and her bikini were unmistakably European. American women (thought Colly) kept *something* back. The top half began fractionally above her nipples; these were clearly visible, in form and almost in colour, under the clinging stuff. The bottom half, the smallest Colly had ever seen, was stretched tight and revealing in front, and clung wispily to her neat white buttocks.

Colly licked his lips.

'*Drinking* time.'

Colly had seen Nigel Heywood's one blurred photograph of his girl. He had not brought it: if anyone searched him and found it his cover would be blown sky-high and he and the girl would be dead very shortly.

No positive identification was possible between the clever, wide-awake face in Nigel's snapshot and this luscious zombie: no more than with Matt. There was no doubt either. No more than with Matt.

'Lunch?' murmured Colly.

'Plenty of time,' cried George.

'Cooking nicely,' said Lyn.

'Good,' said George. They both giggled, as though at a private joke. 'It's the *cocktail* hour.'

Bottles kept appearing from the locker under the blue cushions of the saloon. Under the beady eyes of George and

Lyn, Colly had to drink more than he meant.

Presently he was sitting on a truncated deck-chair under the mizzen boom. Lyn somehow manoeuvred Nikki into his lap. The skin of her thighs felt hot and damp. The skin of her flank and rib-cage was hot and damp under his hand.

He spilt some rum on her shoulder. He licked it up and kissed the shoulder better. George and Lyn applauded gaily.

'This party's *kicking*," cried Lyn.

Nikki wriggled a little and said she was too hot. It was almost the first thing she had said. Her voice was muffled, but to Colly her accent was aggressively upper-class English.

'Not too much sun, dear,' said George.

'Maybe you should go below, dear,' said Lyn.

Then Colly was sitting on the blue-cushioned seat in the saloon, facing another opposite, with a shiny table between. Nikki was leaning against him, breathing a little harshly, her lips wet. It was impossible to tell how much she was taking in.

Lyn had disappeared somewhere below, in the forward part of the yacht. George was on the foredeck, well away from the cockpit, well out of sight of the saloon.

Colly looked blearily round, as though to make sure they were alone. A glint of glass caught his eye, forward, in a place where there was no reason for any glass. The hum of the icebox in the galley sounded very slightly unlike the hum of an icebox.

Colly realised that his face and Nikki's were pouring with sweat.

He was aware of the camera, pointing at him and purring, exposing twenty-four impeccable frames per second.

Nikki moaned. She said: 'Nigel.' She began to kiss Colly.

Colly found this a moment when the call of duty was garbled and difficult to follow.

12

'No *dallying,* lover,' murmured Lyn in the galley forward of the saloon.

Colly Tucker sweated. Nikki sweated. The camera softly hummed.

The new photographer concentrated on his viewfinder. He was only eighteen. He had learned his photography in night-school in Queen's. Sweat poured off his fat forearms. He was hoping to get a tan like Lyn's and George's.

Colly Tucker, at the age of nine, had been summoned to the study of the headmaster of his private school in Massachusetts. He was correctly accused of putting two dozen grasshoppers in the headmaster's desk.

He had providentially and copiously thrown up. The result was not a pardon but at least a useful reprieve.

He had realised the power of mind over stomach.

During the rest of his childhood and adolescence he had summoned the gift at moments of crisis. At home, at school; at summer camp and at dancing-class. Then, at eighteen, it got him out of the embraces of a lecherous old woman. At twenty it got him out of an imminent and deplorable engagement.

Now hot and full of rum he struggled to his feet, his mouth working. He furiously exercised the groggy remnants of his will: he *must* vomit. He lurched up the short companion to the cockpit and afterdeck. He hung over the after rail. He sobbed and retched.

He was out of practice, but it was a fair performance.

George, elegant on the foredeck, looked at him with chagrin. Nicola, in the saloon, moaned. Lyn said, 'Chicken!' and told the photographer to stop wasting film.

Colly appeared to pass out on the afterdeck. Nicola went below and lay on her bunk. George crossly started the diesel and steered south towards St George's.

Late in the afternoon Colly stumbled aboard the big schooner *Cressida,* which had motored in at lunchtime.

He seemed to make an astonishing recovery the moment he went below.

The old charter-party had already gone ashore; the new one had not yet arrived. Yes, Colly could be interested in *Cressida* if the owners were minded to sell. Not a new yacht but a fine sea-boat and very, very comfortable.

The advance guard of the new party arrived to say hullo. It was Colly's friend John Millet, a rich idler like himself but not nearly so rich or so idle. He had been cheated of his free cruise in Colly's *Perelandra,* and had consequently made his own expensive arrangements. He was abusive to Colly and they had a drink. The rest of his party was due in a day or two.

Colly could use *Cressida's* radio. He could also if necessary use *Cressida.*

Colly radio'd a charter office several hundred miles to the north. He had something to report. He reported it in terms that the charter-company, and any eavesdropper, would entirely misunderstand. He hoped Sandro would get through quickly.

Colly had been desperately tempted to strike today, out there under the green bluff. But things were too delicately poised; he could not move without Sandro's authority.

At seven-twenty-five he got it, from Nassau and relayed from St Lucia. He was to press ahead and purchase without delay. He could bargain as hard as circumstances warranted. He must pay particular attention to the radio. At least one of the existing crew must be kept, as their local knowledge would be helpful.

'Understood,' said Colly.

He thanked John Millet and the skipper of *Cressida,* and went ashore to confirm his terrible reputation.

His plan was simple. He would go early in the morning to *Campanula,* would apologise to his friendly hosts on the yacht for making such a fool of himself yesterday, and (eyeing their delicious supercargo) would wait for another invitation. They would doubtless take him at once. They would give him a little less rum.

They certainly had guns and probably throwing-knives on board. These would surely be in the saloon or in the cabins below. He would therefore secure the saloon, get Lyn and the photographer (whom he had never seen) in the galley, and then deal with George, unarmed on deck. It was impossible to plan more accurately. It would depend where they all were around noon. Colly doubted if the girl would be of any practical help.

He climbed out of his car at the yacht-basin at nine-thirty and walked with an air of bashfulness towards *Campanula's* berth.

She was not there.

She was clearing the harbour mouth, sails beginning to draw. Once again she sharpened up and turned north.

Colly ran like a madman the thirty yards to where *Cressida* was tied up. He jumped aboard. Even after so short a distance, even early in the day, he was purple and pouring with sweat after his sharp effort in the blazing sun.

He flopped into the saloon, interrupting John Millet's breakfast.

'Skipper? Crew?' he gasped.

'I guess they're around. You being chased by a girl, Colly?'

'Can you get going? Now at once?'

John laid down his knife. 'You are the most ridiculous friend—'

'For the love of God, John.'

There was something in Colly's face which John had never

seen there before. He dropped his fork with a clatter and ran up on deck.

The skipper was startled and seemed disinclined to move. One deck-hand was varnishing, one was coiling spare cordage. Colly almost physically drove them into action. John Millet, looking stunned, supported him.

'Tell you as we go,' panted Colly.

Cressida was big, beamy, awkward in a confined space. Her gangplank and fenders and hawsers were heavy and her sails enormous. By the time she was in the harbour mouth *Campanula* was still visible but a long way away.

'Can you catch her?'

'With a reaching wind, sure,' said the skipper. 'The more it blows the faster we'll be there. If the wind backs, I dunno. Those new sails, modern hull, she can point higher than old *Cressy*. If the wind drops, I dunno. I guess she'd be fast in a light air.'

'Motor?'

'If it comes to motoring she's three knots faster, I guess.'

'Christ.'

'Point *is,* Mr Tucker, do they know we're chasing her?'

'No.'

'Then I guess we'll catch her. In mebbe two hours.'

'Why are we chasing her, Colly?' asked John Millet.

'They have a prisoner on board.'

'Shucks, son. You been reading Rip Kirby.'

'A girl. Believe me.'

In Colly's face there was again that unfamiliar expression, tense and vengeful. John Millet believed him.

'Get me aboard. Then sail away fast.'

'Want me to come?'

'No.'

The big square topsail was shaken out. *Cressida* responded like a horse to the spur. Her angle of heel increased and she drove through the swell, spray crashing over the weather bow.

Campanula was already growing very gradually larger in the binoculars Colly found in the saloon.

The wind veered, backed, faded, gusted through gaps in the mountains to the east. The pale fan of their wake zigzagged across the sea – this was no time for sailing by the compass, but for getting all possible speed out of the splendid old yacht.

'Don't let *Campanula* get too far upwind.'

'I get you. These damned mountains.'

A black cloud rushed downwind over the island. They could see the wall of rain running over the sea towards them. It hit them with an almost solid impact, roaring on *Cressida*'s deck, soaking them to the skin in the first second. The noise and the stinging assault of the rain confused the senses.

The black cloud swam on as quickly as it came. The rain stopped abruptly. The sun blazed down on them. The wind whipped at their saturated shirts and the great grey sails and dried them quickly.

Campanula was nearer.

'Why, it's Mr *Tucker.*'

'How're you *feeling,* Mr Tucker?'

It was eight minutes after twelve. *Cressida* and *Campanula* were sailing at four or five knots, lifting to the swell, side by side, two fathoms apart. George was at *Campanula*'s wheel and John Millet at *Cressida*'s – two competent and alert helmsmen who knew what they were doing. Lyn stood, relaxed and elegant, by *Campanula*'s lee rail. He held the slack main backstay with one hand and a boathook with the other. He had already slung out three portside fenders.

'Trying out the schooner, Mr Tucker? How does she sail?'

'She's a witch,' said Colly. 'Got one big drawback, though.'

'Yeah?' shouted George. 'What's that?'

'No girls.'

'Come *aboard,* Mr Tucker! It's *party* time!'

'You sure,' said John Millet softly, 'you don't want me along, Colly?'

'No thanks, chum. As soon as I'm aboard her, port your helm and get the hell out.'

'But it's party time, you selfish bastard.'

Colly laughed. His eyes were not laughing.

Nicola came on deck in her lascivious bikini.

John whistled softly. 'You *selfish bas*tard.'

Both helmsmen pointed high, pinching, slowing their ships. All the sails began to quiver and thud. The yachts kept minimum steerage-way, just short of irons.

Lyn galloped up *Campanula's* shrouds and took a nylon line over the main crosstrees. He came down the stay hand over hand like an acrobat, then coiled the line and threw it across the narrow gap of water to Colly. Colly nodded, gestured, grinned, and tied a bowline in the rope. He put the loop over his shoulders and climbed on to *Cressida's* rail. He was now wearing swimming-trunks and a towelling shirt.

Cressida's skipper watched all this jolly by-play with disapproval. He slung out fenders, and perched himself outside the rail on *Cressida's* weather side ready to use his foot to fend off *Campanula*.

Lyn took up the slack in Colly's lifeline. George and John Millet brought the two big yachts still closer together. Colly jumped, easily clutching and catching *Campanula's* rail. He climbed inboard and wriggled out of the loop of rope. He was not much hampered by the gun under his left armpit. He turned and waved to *Cressida:* 'See you this evening, fellers! Thanks for the ride.'

John Millet waved and spun *Cressida's* wheel. The schooner sheered off fast, her sails filling. She showed her splendid high stern to *Campanula* and then her port quarter. Colly heard John shout: 'Ready jibe,' faintly over the noise of wind and water. *Cressida's* crew sprang to sheets and backstays. In seconds she was sweeping away from them to the south.

'Very forgiving of you guys,' said Colly.

'Better *luck* today, Mr Tucker.'

Colly caught Nicola's eye. She was standing, in a pose of boredom, on the starboard deck, holding the shrouds. There was a flicker of dopey recognition on her face. There was perhaps a flicker of tension, perhaps fright, perhaps appeal, perhaps relief.

'Say, uh,' said Colly to George, I'll just go below, use the head, if that's all right.'

'Be our *guest*. Lyn be ready with a *drink* pretty soon.'

Colly had no need of the heads. He had a great need to get below, neutralise the photographer, and command the saloon.

He went down the three steps into the saloon. He winked at Nicola before he disappeared. She showed no reaction. She could be discounted as a tactical factor, for or against.

The saloon door was held open by a brass hook. Colly nudged this as he went by, lurching as though residually a little drunk from the night before. The door swung indecisively with the motion of the yacht, then slammed shut as *Campanula* heeled to a gust.

Colly noisily opened the after door in the saloon. A companion led to the after cabins, between which were head, shower, small aluminium wash-basin. He banged the door shut again, but stayed on the saloon side of it. He crawled quickly forward, out of sight of anyone on deck who might be looking in through the ports. When he reached the forward door he got his gun out of the shoulder-holster and cocked it. Then he opened the door, went through it, and closed it again in one smooth movement. He held the gun in his left hand.

A pale, tubby youth with an outdated Presley hair-do stood in the galley. He was busy bolting a movie-camera to the ironwork of the stove.

He looked up with a knowing, guttersnipe smile, doubtless expecting Lyn. At the sight of Colly and Colly's gun his smile dropped off as though unhooked from his nose and allowed to fall to the deck. His eyes opened wide. His mouth opened and he began to make a little high keening noise.

Colly spoke quietly but very distinctly: 'Listen hard, boy. I don't have the slightest objection to shooting you in the leg or the belly or the back.'

'I'm only eighteen,' whimpered the photographer.

'Too young to die,' said Colly affably. 'Do exactly like I say, will you?'

'Yeah, yeah. I just do what they say. I don't even *look*.'

'Okay. Now listen.' Colly gave the boy orders, made sure he understood them, made as sure as possible, by means of sadistic threats, that he would obey them.

He gestured the boy through the door into the saloon, and followed him. The boy trotted aft, holding the saloon table to keep his balance on the steeply heeling deck. Colly followed, crouching. When the boy opened the after door to the cockpit Colly was beside it, flat against the bulkhead, the gun in his right hand.

'Lynwood! The guy passed out!'

'Oh great,' sighed Lyn on deck.

'Go see,' came George's voice.

Colly heard or imagined a small, despairing exclamation from the girl.

Lyn came delicately down the short companion. He poked his neat blond head into the saloon. 'In here, Albie?' He came lazily in.

The boy suddenly shouted: 'Look out!'

As Lyn spun round Colly clubbed him with the gun. Lyn fell. He rolled down the steep deck to the side of the saloon. Colly turned his gun on the boy. The boy screamed and backed. The back of his knees met the edge of the seat and he collapsed backwards. Colly was suddenly on top of him and he screamed again. With reluctance, and disliking it, Colly hit him on the side of the head with the gun-butt and he crumpled sideways, down from the seat to the deck, and across the deck to the legs of the table.

Now George. But the damage was done.

153

Colly felt the yacht spin to starboard and heard the thunder of flapping sails. She was in irons. George had left the wheel. Did he have an armoury on deck?

'George,' called Colly, imitating the boy's voice as well as he could, 'George, come quick.'

Nicola screamed, close over his head, and then her scream was cut off into a shuddering gasp.

Christ.

Nothing could be seen out of the saloon portholes. Nothing could be heard over the monstrous flapping of the sails. There was no way on deck except by the cockpit.

Every second he stayed down here gave George more time to do whatever he was doing.

George was somewhere forward of the cockpit. He'd have good cover from the mainmast, galley ventilator, forward hatch, or the dinghy on the foredeck. But he might not have a gun.

Colly eased up the steps and peered with infinite caution forward over the roof of the saloon.

A flash of silver bloomed in the corner of his eye and a knife whammed into the mizzen. It hit the steel sleeve of the roller-reefing on the boom, and spun off into the sea. Nicola screamed again, and again her scream was cut off into a gurgle.

Main and mizzen booms swung idly from side to side. The yacht pitched and rolled as she drifted astern. The slack sails rattled overhead.

George was not trying to hide. He stood by the main backstay, slightly crouched so that he could see under the main boom. His right arm was hooked round the stay. His left arm held Nicola in a stranglehold, his forearm against her windpipe and his hand braced behind her shoulder. Her body was in front of his, hiding all but head and arms. In his right hand was a flick-knife with a five-inch blade. Its point was just touching Nicola's rib-cage.

The yacht shuddered and the knife-point pricked Nicola's skin. Nicola tried to scream again but George tightened his left arm against her throat and strangled the scream. There was a smear of blood on Nicola's side.

Her bikini top had slipped off or been pulled off. It flapped round her thighs. The bottom had been torn in her brief struggle with George. It hung down from her left leg and the wind plucked at it and set it dancing in front of her knee.

Her eyes were wide open and aware and terrified. Her mouth was open and her tongue protruded. She was fighting for air against the hard bone and muscle of George's forearm.

In a dead calm, in a dry dock, there was no chance of hitting what Colly could see of George.

'If I was in your position, Mr Tucker,' shouted George over the noise of the flapping sails, 'I'd shoot the girl and then I'd shoot me. But you're a chivalrous gentleman, Mr Tucker, so I guess you won't shoot the girl. In fact, Mr Tucker, there isn't a goddam thing you can do.'

Colly said nothing. There was nothing to say. George was right.

13

Campanula was drifting south-west, and could do so with perfect safety for a hundred miles – or, if she missed Los Testigos, two hundred, to the coast of Venezuela. Lyn and the kid would surface in a few minutes, an arsenal under their hands.

Colly looked back on his mistakes and cursed himself.

He should have slugged the photographer in the galley, then lured Lyn below by bleating in his own voice – lured him right below, to the cabins – and knocked him out there. The kid's courage or loyalty or panic had torn everything up and landed him in this ridiculous impasse.

Time was on George's side. The deadlock must be broken, and fast.

Nicola's body was pink-gold and white, except for the mushroom-brown of her nipples and the black of her pubic hair, and the shreds of bikini fluttering round her legs in the wind, and the red smear of blood under her right breast. George's strangling-arm and his knife-arm and the visible half of his face were a deep mahogany, and hard-muscled. The point of the knife swung as their clamped bodies swung with the roll of the yacht – two inches from Nicola's ribs, then touching and pricking her delicate pink-gold skin.

If Lyn came up on deck with a gun in his hand then Colly would be dead and Nicola no better off than before. They might even let the photographer have her, as a reward.

The deadlock must be broken, and fast.

Colly shrugged. 'Guess you're right, George.'

He let his shoulders droop, in defeat and dejection. He let his gun sag. He backed to the mizzen-mast, and slumped against it, within reach of the wheel.

What he planned put Nicola's life in peril and (since it might not work at all) his own. The alternative was certain death for him and hopeless degradation and hard-drug addiction for Nicola.

'Don't go shooting Lyn when he comes up, Mr Tucker, please,' shouted George politely. 'I don't *want* I should have to make holes in Nikki.'

Because of the jagged land-mass to the east, the wind varied as much (Colly thought) as twenty points. It was hard to anticipate the direction of the gusts. But this was what he must do.

He was still full in George's sight, perhaps as far down as mid-thigh.

'I'll make you a proposition, George,' shouted Colly.

At the same time he groped with his right heel for the spokes of the wheel.

'I can't remember any of you or the name of this yacht. Neither can the girl.'

This needed to be done very quickly.

'That's just crappy talk, Mr Tucker, and you know it.'

A wave knocked *Campanula's* bows to starboard. She heeled a little and the booms swung.

'George, I don't believe Nikki can remember anything!'

A compensating wave nudged *Campanula's* bows to port. A gust caught her headsail. The booms were as far to starboard as the sheets let them go, nudging the weather backstays.

'Listen, George, be reasonable,' shouted Colly in a shrill and pleading voice.

He heaved upwards with his right heel, turning the wheel to starboard. As she drifted astern, rapidly now, the rudder swivelled her head further to port. The booms began to swing.

Anything could happen. Maybe this was a deadlock-breaker.

Possibly the sails would suddenly fill and the yacht heel steeply until she got steerage-way forward. This might make George stagger and give Colly the chance of a shot. It might make him relax his left-arm stranglehold and Nicola might wriggle away from him.

What happened was more savage and complete.

The headsail sheets were snaking over the foredeck, the blocks rattling on the varnished hatch-cover. They caught the anchor-winch, tying the heel of the sail hard down to the deck amidships. The wind thrust hard on the bows, swivelling the yacht to port as though the keel was a pivot. *Campanula* heeled steeply and spun off the wind. The two booms crashed across the deck. The main boom thunked into the side of George's head and he went straight over the rail, which was almost awash.

He took Nicola with him.

Colly spun the wheel amidships and ran forward to free the headsail sheet. The yacht came up into the eye of the wind again and the sails thundered. Colly found the line which had helped him aboard. Feverishly he tied it to a lifebelt and threw the lifebelt overboard.

Campanula was already drifting astern of the two people in the water.

Colly ran to the bows. Nicola was feebly thrashing. George was floating half awash. His skull was split wide open. As Colly watched he sank out of sight. So did Nicola.

Colly tore off his shorts and dived and swam the few strokes to the place. He flipped up his legs and dived down.

He grabbed Nicola's hair and dragged her to the surface. She flapped feebly.

'Relax!' he shouted. 'Relax!'

Campanula was drifting away from them.

Colly rolled over on his back, got the wriggling and naked girl in a loose full-nelson, and kicked furiously.

He glanced over his shoulder after a maniac eternity of violent effort. The yacht's bows seemed no nearer.

He swam on, an armless backstroke, the girl heavy as lead.

Blood from the crunched ruin of George's skull would be drifting downwind. Down at them. God knew how soon the first barracuda would smell it.

Curtains, thought Colly idiotically.

He felt a nudge – something hard between his shoulder-blades. Driftwood? Might help. He half turned and groped backwards with his left arm.

It was the lifebelt, drifting more slowly than the yacht and now at the fullest extent of its rope.

'Nicola! Can you hear? Nicola!'

The girl moaned. Shock, dope, cold. She was making it no easier for Colly.

'Help me get this over your head!'

She seemed to understand. She could hardly help. They were rushing through the water after the drifting bulk of the yacht, at the end of the taut rope. The waves seemed enormous; they were hauled through them. Colly managed to grab the rope and manhandle Nicola's shoulders through the lifebelt. He dared not let go of the rope or of the girl. He had no free hand to pull her arms clear of the lifebelt so that she would float with her head clear. It seemed likely that he would drown her with the effort.

His head began to thud. Waves sucked and crashed round them. He heaved with utter and final desperation, forcing Nicola's limp and slippery body, against the pull of the sea, into the blessed circle of the lifebelt. When she was well inside it he could hold girl and lifebelt with one arm and with the other pull her arms so that the lifebelt fitted under her armpits.

Her long black hair streamed back into the sea, and then after a wave clung all over her face.

If she was still alive they'd done it. Colly pinched the soft flesh of her upper arm sharply between his fingernails. She gave a little high whimper.

They'd done it.

Colly hung to the rope, his breath rasping, his limbs like over-cooked spaghetti. Then he began to haul himself and the lifebelt and Nicola towards *Campanula's* high white side.

The problem of getting up it could be faced when they got there.

They reached the smooth vertical hull, and the water seemed gentler and less hostile. Colly worked a bight of his beloved rope through the lifebelt in front of Nicola and between her cold soft breasts.

'Can you understand?' he shouted.

'Yes,' said Nicola with unexpected clarity.

'I'm going to tie you to this lifebelt.'

'My rubber ring,' said Nicola, giggling weakly.

'Then you're okay for a while, right? Then I'll climb aboard and get the ladder down, and help you up. Right?'

'Why?'

'What d'you mean, *why}*'

'Why? Who are you? What's happening?'

'I'm a friend of Nigel's.'

Nicola suddenly began to cry. Her tears were not visible in the waves which lapped round her face and washed her hair over her eyes and then back and then over her eyes and mouth: but she sobbed quietly.

'Everything's fine,' said Colly. 'Be quick as I can.'

He hoped he had the strength to climb up the rope.

He took it slowly, bracing the soles of his feet on the hull and going up the rope hand over hand. He glanced down. Nicola seemed all right. She was looking up at him anxiously. Colly grinned at her and grabbed *Campanula's* rail. He climbed the rail and collapsed on to the deck. Then he stood up wearily and began unhooking the ladder from its spring-loaded clamps. 'What *did* you do with George, Mr Tucker?' Colly looked up. Lyn was standing four feet away, holding Colly's gun.

14

Colly could take no more from these people. They were disgusting. He was fed up with them. He was suddenly in a blinding, berserk rage.

He therefore did the most foolish thing of his life: he simply threw himself at Lyn, hitting him square in the stomach with his head.

The gun went off. A hole appeared in the flapping mainsail. The gun skidded along the deck and over the side into the sea.

Lyn was winded. Colly hit him on the side of the neck and then on the chin with a right. Lyn crumpled. He was not knocked out. Colly stood over him. Lyn cowered and huddled into the foetal position.

Colly looked over the side. Nicola's face, directly below him in the sea, was shocked and terrified. He waved cheerfully. 'Be right with you.'

He pulled Lyn to the foot of the mainmast, then picked up the coiled main halyard and lashed Lyn to the mast.

He sighed. All this was wasting time. He wanted to go north. He wondered where the photographer was.

The photographer's head now peeped over the top of the saloon. His eyes were like saucers.

'Can you sail this yacht, kid?' said Colly.

'No.'

'Then you need me. If you're holding anything drop it and come here.'

The boy came. He looked scared and groggy. His hands were

empty.

'Now what?'

Colly had to get the ladder over the side, and quick. He dared not leave this punk, however cowed at the moment, in command of the deck.

The thought of Nicola, whimpering and terrified in the water below, nerved him for the uncongenial job. He hit the photographer on the point of the jaw, and then in the solar plexus. He lashed him to the foot of the mizzen-mast with the mizzen halyard.

Adrenalin drained away and he felt overwhelmed with lassitude. He contemplated the idiocy of his charge at Lyn, and the risk he took assuming that the boy would come towards him unarmed. Sandro would not have approved. Colly didn't approve himself. He yawned.

He forced himself to hinge back a yard of rail, slide the ladder into position and lower its claws into the brass sockets in the gunwale, and climb down to get Nicola.

'Gun?' mumbled Nicola.

'Don't worry about a single thing. We're off to meet Nigel and a girl you know called Jenny.'

Nicola nodded meekly.

Colly got her on to the bottom rung of the ladder. She was incapable of climbing up. Hauling on the line tied to the lifebelt he somehow, after a long time, with care and labour, got her shivering and helpless nakedness on to the deck.

He looked at the time on the chronometer, 12.29. Exactly twenty-one minutes since he came aboard *Campanula*. He thought the chronometer must be broken. Its hands moved, just perceptibly, convincingly. Twenty-one minutes.

He got Nicola below and dried her, and put her into a bunk and wrapped her up. She was weak and her teeth were chattering, but she was not a zombie. Her marvellous body, now that she was no longer a zombie, excited Colly. He envied Nigel.

'My pills,' she said.

'Where are they?'

'I don't know. You must find them! Please! I'll do anything!'

'Easy, Nicola. I'll get this tub sailing, then we'll look around.'

'I'll do anything!' She sat up and the blankets fell from her breasts. *I'll do anything.*

Colly swallowed. Two hundred miles of this.

'As soon as we're sailing,' he said. 'I promise. Relax now like a good girl.'

Immediately afterwards *Campanula* was once again sailing briskly northwards.

Colly checked the headsail, main and mizzen sheets, the strength and direction of the wind, and the course. Then he lashed the wheel.

He checked the knots which held Lyn to the mainmast and the photographer to the mizzen. Lyn looked down, avoiding his eye. The boy was groggy.

He went below and searched for pills. He did not like the idea of cramming Nicola still fuller of evil chemicals. At the same time he could not cut her off suddenly. A ravening addict on this yacht was one problem too many. Her ultimate cure was Nigel's affair.

The pills were in a drawer in the chart-table, with two guns, a small number of cigarettes and an unopened box of sterilised disposable syringes.

The pills were diamorphine. There was also a fair quantity of what Colly took to be heroin hydrochloride.

Colly gave Nicola half as much as she said she needed, on the grounds that addicts, like alcoholics, always lie. Shortly afterwards she went to sleep and Colly set about getting lunch.

During the afternoon he offered Lyn the alternative of staying exactly where he was, indefinitely, without food or water: or talking.

Lyn talked.

Campanula belonged to a Mr Henry Body. Who was American, yes. Who was the boss, yes.

The operation was doubling up, yes. There was a new yacht. *What was the new yacht? Where was she?*

Lyn knew nothing about the new yacht. Nothing. Nothing at all. Mr Tucker could do what he liked. Lyn could tell him nothing.

Colly checked helm, compass, sheets, stays. He was not thinking about any of them. He was sickened by the necessity of disbelieving a man who was quite likely telling the truth. Of trying to get information out of him which he just didn't have.

Only the thought of Jenny in Mr Body's hands and on Mr Body's yacht nerved him for the business.

Nigel's big dark man had used a cigarette. Okay, a cigarette. There were hundreds of methods and Colly loathed them all.

Quite soon Lyn talked.

The new yacht was called *Sandalshoon*. Owned by Mr Body. At Antigua. Ready to go.

Colly went to the radio.

Seventy minutes later he got Sandro's crackling and distorted voice.

He named the new yacht he wanted to buy. He named its owner and present location.

Afterwards Colly let Nicola talk to Nigel. Her face came alive and she said that she would marry Nigel.

Lyn talked more freely after Colly convinced him that George was dead.

Mr Body had bought *Campanula* two or three years before. Lyn had been with her for eighteen months; George had joined earlier. Matt Warren was the fifteenth victim. Lyn remembered the names of some of the others. It was clear that he despised the marks for their lust and drunkenness and grossness, and had no compunction about the outcome. He was himself a near-teetotaller, only an occasional smoker and a pure-food fanatic with a hatred of chemical fertilisers.

Mr Body was rich and came from New York. He had property in Florida. He spent a fair amount of time in the Caribbean. Lyn knew nothing else about him.

There had been seven girls. Lyn knew that they were British and on dope of one sort or another. They mostly had Canadian passports. Lyn had no idea if the passports were genuine, or if the names in them were right. He had not asked any questions about Mr Body or about the girls.

One of the girls had been killed by Matt Warren. One had been drowned accidently, when drunk. One had drowned herself. The others had been taken away by George, on instructions from Mr Body. Lyn had no idea where they went or what happened to them. He did not comment on Colly's suggestion that they were murdered because their usefulness was ending.

George had killed the previous photographer. Lyn had had nothing to do with this, and did not know the reason. Maybe he stepped out of line with a girl.

He understood that the girls were all registered addicts and were supplied with drugs legally under British law. He would not otherwise have consented to give them drugs, which he despised.

Lyn was paid about eight times a normal deck-hand's salary, and he lived free. The money went into a New Jersey bank on the first of every month.

The photographer was called Albert Joy. He had been approached at home by a Mr Feld at the end of February, given a passport and some money, and flown to Antigua via Bermuda. It was his first job. He had only ever seen the one girl. He had hardly spoken to her. He had only used the camera once, when Colly came aboard at St George's. He knew nothing about any drugs or any blackmail or any other girls.

Colly found that Nicola, after her rest and some food, was perfectly capable of taking the wheel and also of pointing a pistol. She covered Lyn while Colly untied his hands, and sailed *Campanula* while Lyn ate and drank. They repeated the procedure with Albie Joy.

Colly anchored for the night in shallow water in the Central Grenadines. They had made excellent time.

Nicola whimpered for her fix, but she was now ashamed. She wore slacks and a shirt and she was much, much better.

She remembered nothing between standing naked in a cold bare room on a foggy February night in London, and being in this yacht in a hot harbour with other yachts. She cried when Colly told her about Nigel and Sandro and Jenny.

The days of waiting had been awful for Sandro.

He had brought Nigel to Barbados, from which the whole long string of the Windward and Leeward Islands could be most easily reached. They stayed at a small dull hotel and tried to relax. They had plenty of sun and a little sailing. Sandro turned almost black; his blue eyes looked like some absurd but charismatic mistake. Nigel tanned more reluctantly; he was in danger of burning. Sandro was strict with him. A burnt instep or ankle is virtually disabling. 'Sunburn,' he said, 'is a self-inflicted wound according to British military law. So also in my law.'

The days crawled by. They could do nothing. Until Colly's noisy reputation attracted a certain white ketch, and it came for him, and he hijacked it, and he secured the necessary information, by any means he chose, from its crew.

When their routine call on the maritime waveband gave them Colly's news, Sandro felt like a watch that has been overwound: so tense, so charged with power, that he was in danger of popping.

At least he now had some faith in his lieutenant. Nigel had changed from a dull Londoner into a companion; his brief and crackling conversation with his girl changed him further, into the semblance of a soldier.

They flew to Antigua, fitting on to a packed B.O.A.C. 707. They bumped, by night, the length of the island to English Harbour, in an Austin taxi. They checked into a hotel booked from Barbados, then took the taxi on, round an enormous salt-marsh, to the yacht-basin.

No *Sandalshoon.*

'Went out this morning,' a yacht skipper told them. 'Owner seemingly has a house at Coral Bar. *Sandalshoon's* there, I guess.'

'I pray tomorrow still,' murmured Sandro.

They dined on a stone terrace under the stars. A steel band of ten-year-olds giggled and bonged, not quite drowning the tree-frogs. People danced – scarlet-faced, casually dressed, loudly friendly.

'The Coral Bar Colony,' said Sandro thoughtfully. 'I think we look first from the land. It may be that we need go no further than this Mr Body's house.'

'Do you think Jenny's there?'

'Yes.'

'Maybe the yacht's gone there to collect her.'

'I think obvious.'

'Christ. We're just in time.'

'If we are in time, *caro.*'

They bumped north along a road through dusty scrub and then, on higher ground, through sugar-plantations.

'No sugar now,' said the driver. 'Only a small bit. They import sugar now for the rum.'

'Uneconomic?' said Nigel.

'Ah, sir.'

They went through a village of neat, minute houses propped high above the ground on stones. 'Prosperity Village. My village.'

They exclaimed politely. The little houses were covered in bougainvillaea and the gardens blazed with hibiscus. 'We won third prize for the bes' kep' village.'

They passed a small ornate church – an orange corrugated-

167

iron roof, rose-pink decorated plaster. 'Our church. The Pentecostal Church.'

The village straggled along several hundred yards of road. Children were everywhere; their clothes varied from neat muslin dresses with brilliant sashes to vests which stopped at the waist. The driver tooted and waved as they drove past his neighbours. Plump ladies in straw hats decorated with flowers raised benign, pink-palmed hands as they rattled by.

'I never been *inside* the Coral Bar Colony,' said the driver.

'Nor have I?' said Nigel, a note of interrogation in his voice.

'Movie-stars from America. They have a *golf*-course.'

'Do many yachts go there?'

'Nowhere yachts can go. *Yachts* go to English Harbour. Ah sir, golf-course, and the *houses*. My cousin Herbert, he's electrician, he put the *wires* in one house. *He* never saw nothin' like it. Coral Bar,' announced the driver as the car slowed down. 'They expectin' you, sir?'

They drew up at a gate – a single hinged pole like a level-crossing. A man in a peaked cap came out of a small stone building like a blockhouse.

A small sign said: 'Coral Bar Colony. Strictly Private.' The road visible beyond the gate, curving down between dry and spiky vegetation towards the sea, was in sharp contrast to the public road they had been travelling: broad, well-metalled, neatly edged.

'Yes, sir?' said the guard. His ebony face was thin and his cheek-bones high. His shoulders were enormously broad. His expression was placid. He made no attempt to raise the bar.

Sandro leaned out of his window. 'Can you tell me if Miss Olivia Winstanley has arrived?'

'No member of that name, sir.'

'No no, she will be staying with a member. Her yacht is coming here, the, ah, *Wapshott Castle."*

The gateman looked at him expressionlessly.

'Can you tell me if a Miss Winstanley is staying with a member here?'

'No guest of that name, sir.'

'Perhaps I could have a word with someone at the office.'

'I can't let you in, sir. There is an absolute rule. You must have a note, a letter.'

'Perhaps I can use your telephone to talk to the office.'

'No telephone here, sir.'

This seemed to be untrue. Wires ran downhill from the blockhouse.

'I will send a note, then,' said Sandro.

'Ah, sir.'

'Too ridiculous,' said Nigel for their driver's benefit as they ignominiously drove away. 'Olivia should have left a message.'

'The *Castle* is perhaps not here yet. She is a madwoman. I am inclined to refuse to go on her stupid yacht.'

So they fulminated, and the taxi took them back to the Planters' Tavern.

'Mighty fussy, Coral Bar,' said their driver in a tone of pity.

'Tomorrow,' said Sandro, 'we will take a little cruise in a boat. More than anything I hope Jenny is not quite full of drugs.'

Jenny was pretty full of all kinds of things.

She dimly saw, as an episode involving a girl she once knew, a picture of herself standing naked under a bright light. A tiny, distant picture, seen through the wrong end of a telescope. There were blurred pictures laid over this, sightless sensations, of obscene investigating hands and of waves of sleep.

She was unaware of plastic and paint, of customs-clearance or air-freighting, of an amateur but adequate medical examination in a small house near Miami, of black plastic and paint being peeled off her body and reduced to anonymous ashes in an incinerator.

Lucidity of a kind had come back to her as she lay, tied, in the back of a Pontiac wagon on the way to Miami Airport. She was aware of flying.

A much greater lucidity had followed during the dusty drive across Antigua from St John's. She kept her face close to the open window. A little colour came back into her cheeks. There was very little strength in her arms and legs. She realised she was half starved. She realised she was a prisoner, a hostage, a slave in the hands of people who knew who she was and knew she was an enemy.

Beside her in the back seat of the Dodge was a tough dark man with dense dark fuzz on the backs of his hands.

Charming, thought Jenny muzzily.

They came to a gate with a blockhouse.

The guard in the peaked cap let the Dodge through his gate without hesitation. He made a sketchy salute to the back seat. The bar clanged down behind them. The tyres of the Dodge whispered over the fine new road downhill towards the ocean.

They passed a number of houses on the hillside. These were long and low, with big windows and verandas and luscious gardens. Harold, the driver, gave them an awestruck commentary. It was like a conducted bus-tour of Beverly Hills – every house seemed to belong to a resounding Hollywood name.

Nothing more public, nothing more respectable could be imagined.

They stopped in front of a house at least as large, airy and gracious as those they had seen. It was made of white-painted wood and rough grey stone; the roof was all silvery slats of weathered greenheart. A gardener in a straw hat was picking up fallen blossoms, one by one, and putting them delicately into a basket.

Harold carried some bags to the shady porch. A motherly Negress in a lace cap came out on to the porch and gestured welcomingly. The nondescript man beside Jenny, who had hardly spoken six words since Miami, helped her out of the car and into the house.

She took little careful steps and leaned on him heavily.

The Negress was all smiles and gushing concern. 'Bein' British, *you'll* want *tea,* mistress.' Jenny was taken into a high white bedroom and lowered into a cane chair. The door closed and she was left alone. She heard a key turn in the lock. She saw that the windows were barred.

Through the window she saw her nondescript companion get back into Harold's car. The car drove away up the hill.

Tea came, excellent Orange Pekoe. It was not drugged. There were biscuits and little cakes, which Jenny wolfed.

She tiptoed to the looking-glass, and was revolted by what she saw. Pony-tail, white lipstick, pounds of mascara, a skirt inches longer than she was used to.

Feet shuffled in the tiled passage outside. She nipped back to the cane chair and subsided into it and closed her eyes.

It was important not to appear to need too many massive hypodermic shots of anything.

15

'I'm very, very pleased to welcome you, Lady Jennifer,' said a man with a tiny head.

Jenny swivelled her head slowly and seemed to focus with an effort. 'Mm?'

The motherly housekeeper had helped her, in the early evening, along the passage to the sitting-room. Jenny was nearly certain that the housekeeper was innocent – had been told about a mental illness or a suicide attempt.

The sitting-room was charming. Wide doors with fine mesh screens opened on to the veranda. The remains of tea for three was daintily spread on a table on the veranda; a pair of yellow birds pecked at the sugar bowl. In the hibiscus beyond the balustrade a humming-bird darted into trumpet after trumpet. Then the ground fell away steeply and the sea gleamed between coconut-palms.

There were three men in the room.

One stood by the door. He wore faded blue cotton shirt and trousers and faded espadrilles. He was young, tanned, unmistakably English. He was not obviously guarding the door, merely standing beside it. It was clear to Jenny that he would not have let her through the door.

The second stood by the screen-door giving on to the veranda. He was thin and dark; he might have been Spanish. He wore a shirt like an imitation Fred Perry tennis-shirt over very tight black jeans. His feet were bare. He would not have let Jenny out on to the veranda if she had tried to dash for the veranda.

The third man, the man who had spoken, sat exactly in the middle of a chintz-covered sofa. He was slightly over middle height, with a muscular medium build. Jenny guessed he was fifty, but he looked ageless. His face was extraordinarily smooth and healthy. He was lightly tanned. His eyes were clear and blue. He looked like a man with no vices. He spoke like an American, but an American who had spent much time in Britain, a member of a cultured, sophisticated, East Coast minority.

The smallness of his head amounted to a deformity. There was a little sandy hair on his doll-like skull.

He went on: 'You haven't been well, Jennifer. Our friends in London were worried. I hope you'll agree we all did the right thing, bringing you here. You'll have a lot of fun. Nobody stays sick in a place as beautiful as this.'

'Mm,' said Jenny.

'That's my girl. Now I very much want you to meet my friends Ricky,' he indicated the Englishman by the door, 'and Chuck.' He waved at the dark man by the veranda.

'Ricky de Malahide,' said the Englishman, bowing slightly and grinning with great charm. 'How do you do?'

'Chuck Running Deer,' said the dark man with a ghost of a smile. 'Hullo, Jennifer.'

'Chuck is skipper of my yacht *Sandalshoon*. Probably the only full-blooded Sioux Indian with a job like that.'

Chuck smiled fleetingly again.

'And Ricky is navigator, crewman, cook—'

'Cabin-boy, bottle-washer, lady's-maid,' finished Ricky with his brilliant grin.

'Mm,' said Jenny.

'You'll like *Sandalshoon*, Jennifer. The best-found ship in the Caribbean, if I do say so. Absolutely brand-new. I alas can only spare a day or two now, then I have to go back to New York for a week on business. But I'm relying on you, dear, to be my guest on board.'

A week, thought Jenny. How many pay-offs from how many desperate men can you fit into a week? How many more new yachts can you buy with the result?

She only said: 'Mm.'

The plump housekeeper brought Jenny some supper in her room. She said her name was Hortensia. She locked the door behind her when she left.

Jenny carefully smelled and tasted the fish-soup and the stew; it was sloppy, invalid food, but she needed it. The soup had a very slight, bitter, chemical tang. It went down the lavatory in the gleaming bathroom which opened off the bedroom. A pity – it looked a rich and nourishing mixture.

With each mouthful of stew Jenny felt strength coming back. But she seemed in a state of comatose collapse when Hortensia came for the plates. Hortensia put her to bed, cooing and fussing.

Her nightdress, like all her possessions, was cheap, anonymous, American, brand-new. Everything she had with her added up to half an hour in any big department store. It was oddly depersonalising, having no single physical object she recognised.

She lay in the dark, listening to the incredible music of the frogs and crickets.

She was aware of misery, of an aching need. She whimpered for whatever kindly forgetfulness she had sent down the lavatory with the soup.

She fought a terrible struggle with herself, to stop herself banging on the locked door and screaming for the drug.

In the morning her hands were shaking; but she poured her coffee down the lavatory.

In the jolly, map-hung hall of the Planters' Tavern there was a framed photograph of a small ketch. Below the photograph a hand-lettered sign read:

'DAY CHARTERS. Aux. Ketch *Hubris*. See the breathtaking coast, the offshore islands, from a *new angle*. United States $15.00 per head. Min. 2 persons. Your host and skipper BILL FOSS.'

Hubris was rather a mess, but Bill Foss sailed her well. He was a lanky Canadian from the Maritimes; he seemed not to enjoy his life.

Sandro and Nigel had collected box-lunches; Bill Foss picked them up from the hotel jetty in his outboard.

Nigel was told what ropes to pull; Sandro seemed to know already. (Bill Foss had no permanent crew; he either pressed his customers into service or sailed single-handed.) They went off under canvas and sailed for two hours on a single tack.

'Coral Bar Colony,' said Bill, pointing at the shore.

They could see the road snaking down the hillside. The houses were hardly visible, having been built to blend in with the landscape. There was an administrative building near the sea, and a short beach.

'Shoal water here,' said Bill. 'Hell of a lot of coral. No chart's up to date more than a year.'

'You can't take her in closer?'

'Nope.'

A yacht was anchored well offshore.

'Ugly bitch,' said Bill. 'Let's take a look.'

He pointed *Hubris* closer to the wind. She heeled more steeply, sailed more slowly. They passed a few fathoms downwind of the anchored yacht.

'*Sandalshoon*. American.'

'She looks brand-new.'

'Maiden voyage,' said Bill. 'Ugly bitch.'

She was a motor-sailer with a grey-green hull. There was something clumsy about her stern and her coachwork looked too high and lavish for the hull. She was ketch-rigged, but the mizzen was nearly as tall as the mainmast; both masts were metal and looked too thick for their length. They were festooned with electronic gadgetry, including radar. An awning was stretched over the mizzen boom. The yacht looked comfortable, seaworthy, and very expensive.

'Twin G.M. diesels. She can shift under power.'

A slim man in faded blue came on deck. He waved to *Hubris*. Bill Foss waved back. Sandro and Nigel were sitting inconspicuously in the cockpit.

A Boston dory with a big outboard was approaching *Sandalshoon* from the shore, from the Coral Bar beach. Sandro raised binoculars.

A fair girl. A man with an oddly small head. Luggage.

The little square tender, almost a hydroplane, was steered by a thin dark man. He roared round in a tight curve, throttled back, and drifted expertly to the foot of the ladder amidships on *Sandalshoon's* port side.

'Coral Bar people,' said Bill Foss. 'Hollywood or Wall Street. You fellows feeling hungry?'

They anchored half an hour later in the lee of Smith's Island. They swam, drank Bill's duty-free gin, ate their sandwiches and headed back.

Sandalshoon was still there. The three men seemed to be dozing under the awning. There was no sign of the girl.

The Charter office had a powerful transmitter for getting messages to its far-flung yachts. Sandro was able to use this at 6 p.m.

He spoke to Colly, far to the south.

Nigel spoke to Nicola.

They were both more cheerful as a result.

'694238,' Sandro finished.

'*694238,*' repeated Colly's distorted voice.

'An American football play,' explained Sandro to the girl in the Charter office. 'A joke. I do not, myself, understand

American jokes.'

'What was that number?' asked Nigel as they sauntered back towards the jetty and Bill Foss's dinghy.

'A coded map reference. We have a rendezvous. Let me think.'

They paused at the edge of the dockyard by an enormous old kedging-anchor, which rust had eaten into the semblance of a fossilised tree.

'We know that *Sandalshoon* is booked to come in here in two days for some screws to be screwed up in her engines. We know that her owner is on board her for the first time, and with a new crew. We know that he is a rich American called Mr Henry Body, who comes here sometimes and has an interest also in another yacht.'

This was all dockyard gossip, undoubtedly accurate.

'We know that General Maxwell is visiting her at eleven tomorrow, there where she is.'

This they had learnt in the office just before Sandro spoke to Colly.

'They will start a two-day cruise, I think? Starting about noon tomorrow? Then the proud owner can play with his new toy. And their pretty passenger will be more healthy and more attractive.'

'And then they're in business.'

'Exactly as you say. Except that they must kill us first. Which is by the way possible. Let me think. When we hit them it must be very quick and complete, and Jenny must not be shot. Now listen very carefully.'

General Maxwell, late Royal Artillery, had retired to a delightful part-time job. He was retained by a number of British travel-agents to look at yachts available for charter. He was not concerned with seaworthiness or sailing qualities so much as with the comfort of the cabins, the food and drink, and the question of personality. A yacht is a very confined space. Everyone knows stories about charter parties that turned sour – wife-swapping, divorces, the acrimonious shattering of lifelong friendships. The General could do nothing about wives; he could take a view about skipper and crew. He was looking for congenial, tactful people who knew how to behave.

Sandalshoon charmed him. Everything was exactly as it should be. He had met the owner once or twice casually at the Admiral's Inn, but of course the owner was not the point. The point was the galley, which was the best the General had ever seen in a yacht of *Sandalshoon's* size; the three charter-cabins aft, roomy, airy, most ingeniously designed; and above all, the skipper and mate.

The General was not one to say: 'Of course some of my best friends are homosexuals,' but he did know enough to regard them highly as servants. Brother-officers had been wonderfully lucky in pansy batmen. They were tidy and tactful, took great pride in domestic management, were often first-class cooks. This Red Indian fellow was presumably a thoroughly competent skipper – Henry Body would hardly entrust a yacht like *Sandalshoon* to a beginner: but quite on top of all that the General could picture candlelight and finger-bowls and well-chosen music, beautifully presented meals, flowers in the cabins – all the gracious touches which the brochures promised and the yachts so often failed to deliver.

The very pretty, very silent girl was apparently a guest, not part of the complement. The General jovially regretted this. Mr Body and his boys laughed and agreed.

'I still can't see,' grumbled Bill Foss, 'why you didn't go with the General. He would have taken you free, and you're paying me thirty bucks.'

'Because the good General has business, Bill. We thought it more *commodo* to come with you. We will see our friend when the General leaves.'

'Why not do all this yesterday?'

'We did not know yesterday that Olivia was on board.'

'That fair chick?'

'The poor thing. She has not been well. I think Mr Body is very kind. We will surprise her.'

'Will the owner be glad to see you?'

Sandro indicated the bottle of French wine, which is very expensive in those parts. 'We bribe him to be delighted.'

Sandalshoon, still at anchor, came into view round the headland.

Ricky brought the General a gin and tonic under the awning, and the four men stood chatting.

'*Hubris,*' said the General, glancing astern and seeing the little ketch in the distance.

'Funny,' said Ricky. 'She came this way yesterday.'

'She's on day charter. She comes up here a lot. The people generally have a picnic lunch on Smith's Island.'

He liked Bill Foss, but he had not felt able to recommend *Hubris* to the travel-agents. Bill was a bit too prickly and opinionated; and finger-bowls in his saloon were about as unlikely as *pâté de foie gras.*

His own little sloop *Bimini* was tied astern of *Sandalshoon,* alongside the Boston dory. Ricky pulled her up to the big yacht by her painter. The General thanked them all and hopped down on to the deck of his boat. Ricky paid out the painter again and stood ready to cast off. The General hoisted his mainsail, which flapped noisily.

Hubris was close to them now. Mr Body, Chuck and Ricky were all watching the General cleat his main halliard and then scramble forward to hoist his jib. None of them noticed that *Hubris* was pinching up very close to the wind – her sails were trembling at the luff and she was hardly moving through the water. None of them saw two figures slip over the gunwale on the lee side.

The General waved. Ricky cast off. The General pulled in his painter, *Bimini* drifted astern, her sails flapping. He got back to his tiller, reversed helm, filled his sails, and went off fast on a broad reach.

With this stiff quartering wind he'd be back in time for a late lunch.

Mr Body, Chuck and Ricky turned inboard. Mr Body picked up a book. Ricky sponged up the damp ring left on the deck by the General's drink; then he started untying the lashings of the awning. Chuck went below.

Hubris had paid off a little. Her sails were drawing and she was travelling well. She was soon some distance away. Glancing at her idly, Ricky took it that the party on board were playing canasta or being sick below; no one was visible except the skipper.

'The ladder will not be there much longer. Look, they get ready to go soon. We move now.'

Nigel gulped and nodded.

They were holding on to the stern of the dory, one each side of the outboard. Round the neck of each was a length of nylon cord which secured the mouth of a waterproof polythene bag.

Nigel was no longer able to believe any of the things which were happening to him. He had never expected to be in the Caribbean, or to have a bag round his neck containing two different guns, or to be about to risk his life in a fight with dangerous gangsters. This was not something he had chosen, a situation in which his will had played any part. He was a leaf on a stream.

He was intensely excited, very frightened, and prepared to kill.

Sandro nodded.

Nigel took a deep breath, duck-dived and swam under water. He saw the dark mass of *Sandalshoon,* and swam on. His lungs felt ready to burst and the polythene bag slithered awkwardly round his body. He surfaced as quietly as he could under the sheer of *Sandalshoon*'s stern. His breath wanted to come in deep, shuddering gasps; he made himself breathe quietly. He glanced towards the dory. No sign of Sandro. He used his palms against the nile-green hull to work himself silently round to the foot of the ladder amidships. He waited, listening hard.

He heard it: a gurgling which was closely similar to the lapping of the water against the hull, but, if you were waiting for it, a distinctive and additional sound.

He began to count to twenty, using the formula for counting in seconds: '*One* higgledy-piggledy, *two* higgledy-piggledy—'

At the same time he lifted himself with infinite caution out of the water on to the ladder, and then with one hand undid the neck of the polythene bag and took out the harpoon-pistol.

This was a weapon which horrified him. Sandro had said it was based on something invented by the Philippino gangs. On to a pistol-grip with a trigger was fixed a nine-inch tube containing a powerful spring. It fired a steel knitting-needle. Its advantages were: it was silent; the needle could be recovered, and the wound would be ascribed to a stiletto; it left no smell or powder-stain; if fired into an arm or leg it disabled, and painfully, but it did not smash and maim like a bullet; but it could kill entirely effectively if you wanted it to and were close.

'*Thirteen* higgledy-piggledy, *fourteen* higgledy-piggledy—'

Bare feet flapped by on the deck, inches from his head. They flapped back.

'*Seventeen* higgledy-piggledy, *eighteen* higgledy-piggledy—'

And suddenly a man was standing at the top of the ladder, in the gap in the rail, looking down at him with an expression of amazement. A slim man, in faded blue.

'Well! Where did *you* spring from? What's that thing?'

Nigel raised the harpoon-pistol and shot the man in the thigh. Inches of steel and the neat little head jutted from the blue cotton cloth. A small red stain started and spread. The man screamed and clutched the place and collapsed backwards.

Nigel scrambled up the rest of the ladder and crouched on the deck, pulling out the other gun. The proper gun, with bullets.

He saw that Sandro was this moment scrambling over the stern, having swarmed most dangerously up the tender's painter.

'Don't move,' said Sandro to the small-headed man in a deck-chair by the wheel.

The man did not move.

'Get below, find the third. Harpoon.'

Nigel nodded, recocking the spring. He ran down into the saloon and into the muzzle of a big automatic.

He stopped.

'Dump your toys, babe,' said the thin-lipped dark man holding the gun. 'Stalemate, Mr Body,' he called.

'Thank you, Chuck.' The man with the tiny head turned lazily to Sandro. 'Do you want both your friends killed, or will you put that thing away and tell me what I can do for you?'

Nigel dropped his gun and then his harpoon-pistol. They fell with a clatter. The jar released the catch on the spring; a steel knitting-needle thudded into the leg of the table and stuck there, vibrating.

'Count Ganzarello and Mr Heywood, I think. How clever of you to find us so quickly. I don't think Lady Jennifer will really be glad to see you, at least not after I've finished with you. She is not, I may point out, any use to you just at the moment. But she will shortly be of great use to me.'

16

It seemed to Nigel that the end of the world had come. The sense of defeat and futility was as awful as the black moment in London when they realised that they had been watching the wrong house for a week.

But Sandro's voice, in the cockpit, was quite bland. 'You take my pawn, Mr Body. I take your king. You will add a hole to the existing holes you have in your ridiculous little head.'

The big muzzle of the gun in the dark man's hand pointed unwaveringly at Nigel's navel. This was a new experience for him and he disliked it. He did not think Sandro would let him be killed. But he knew that if it came to a choice between Jenny and him Sandro would sacrifice him. He did not disagree with this arrangement of values: but it saddened him to think that Nicola, now safe and his and needing him, would only have his corpse.

Jenny was presumably below, either trussed up or doped.

'The very best thing that can happen to you,' said Mr Body, 'is that I shall not kill or mutilate Lady Jennifer. I emphasise, the *very best*. The worst things that can happen are the things I shall cause to be done to her if you try my patience for many more seconds.'

A pale figure appeared behind the man with the gun, in the door of the saloon.

'If you shoot me your boss gets it,' said Nigel.

'Like we said. Stalemate.'

It was necessary to keep the gunman's whole attention. Nigel gabbled on: 'If my boss shoots your boss you shoot me, but then you won't have a boss and *then* my boss might shoot you—'

Jenny brought a full bottle of Gordon's Export gin down on the head of the skipper. He went straight down in a heap, landing hard.

'Stalemate broken,' called Jenny. 'How are you, fatty?'

'Fine, *carissima.*'

'And good for you, Nigel darling. Quite a new role. What would they say in the ad game?'

Nigel grinned. He and Jenny embraced, laughed with relief. Jenny picked up the skipper's gun and handed it to Nigel.

'Watch him for an instant, will you, pet, while I see what Sandro's at.'

Sandro was covering Mr Body with a harpoon-pistol and Nigel's victim with an automatic.

'What is so convenient about yachts is that there is always much rope,' he said. 'How are you truly, Jenny?'

'Full of beans. Now you can teach me sailor's knots.'

They started tying up Mr Body. He suddenly began to struggle like a maniac. Sandro knocked him out with the butt of his pistol.

They extracted the needle from Ricky's thigh, cleaned and dressed the small puncture, and told him cheerfully that wounds never heal in the tropics. He was also bound.

Jenny relieved Nigel in case Chuck woke up, while Nigel and Sandro carried the first two into the saloon. Then they tied up Chuck.

'Very tidy,' said Sandro. 'We must now sail two hundred miles as quickly as we can. We can tell stories as we go.'

Hubris sailed by, three fathoms away. Bill Foss hailed them.

'Hey! You forgot your wine!'

'So we did. Listen, Bill,' shouted Sandro, 'we're staying aboard. We'll send you the money.'

'What do I do with this wine?'

'Drink it!'

Bill Foss waved and sailed on. He had only known Sandro two days, but he knew he would get his money.

Very soon after he was out of sight *Sandalshoon's* anchor was up and she was thudding south under power and sail.

'How did you come up from below?' Nigel asked Jenny.

'On my pins. Left foot right foot. It's funny what loopholes people leave. It's always the way. You only win because other people make bloomers. They just didn't take quite enough trouble to make sure I was getting their drugs. Which meant I missed quite a bit of nourishing scoff. I could hardly lift that gin bottle.'

'Food at once, Nigel,' said Sandro.

'Oh yes, please,' said Jenny. She then fainted.

Sandro gave Nigel the wheel and a compass-course. He put Jenny to bed. Later they fed her on soup and she was able to laugh at herself and come up on deck.

'What will you do for a job?' Jenny asked Nigel.

'Colly says he can fix me up with something out here, if we like. Property or yacht-broking or a pub or something. I'll see what Nicola thinks.'

'I'm so glad about her, love.'

'Yes. Colly can have my guts.'

'You've got some too, darling.'

'This is piracy,' said Mr Henry Body. 'You are in very serious legal trouble.'

'I am quite prepared to add murder to the list of my crimes,' said Sandro. 'Please be quiet while I use your excellent radio.'

A prearranged message went quickly, by a complicated route. It went to English Harbour, then to St John's, then by Telex to the Galactic Studios' London office, then by an uncomprehending and contemptuous Flavia May to Miss Olivia Winstanley.

The message seemed frivolous gibberish. 'That Sandro,' said Flavia May. 'That slob.'

But it sent Miss Winstanley to Scotland Yard and an interview in a depressing office. Some men in felt hats then arrested a big dark man, a shiny gingery man, a sad little man in a woolly-muffler and a pasty-faced man with black paint under his fingernails. The charges included armed assault, attempted murder, actual bodily harm, abduction, defrauding H.M. Customs and Excise, and unauthorised possession of various proscribed drugs. All four were remanded in custody until certain key witnesses, thought to be abroad, should become available.

Other messages, worded by Colly, went to New York and the New Jersey and Florida police.

Mr Body's description meant nothing to anyone.

Ricky de Malahide, in some pain from his wounded thigh, said that he had been hired by the Red Indian skipper and vetted by Mr Body, whom he had not previously met. He had been a male model in London and New York, had drifted south to the sun, and had made a modest living as a waiter and then as a steward and deck-hand in various yachts. Any views he might have formed about the set-up in *Sandalshoon* were pure speculation. He knew they were picking up a cook in a day or two, he thought an Italian. He had heard that this Italian was a good photographer, which interested him because of his own professional background.

Chuck Running Deer, in some pain from the blow on his head, said he had been hired by the skipper of Mr Body's other yacht and vetted by Mr Body, whom he had not previously met. He had grown up in California, in San Diego, and had never been interested in anything except the sea. He had served in merchant ships and cruise ships and held a second mate's certificate.

He clearly knew rather more than his English crewman, but Sandro guessed that his pain threshold would be high and that he would give nothing away.

Mr Henry Body laughed in their faces. He challenged them to prove anything against him, to link him with any blackmailing, any suicides, the deaths of any policemen. He challenged them even to find out who he was. Looking at the back of his tiny skull Jenny wanted to smash it. Sandro shared this feeling but said that they should wait.

They flew south in front of the trade-wind and Sandro decided to sail all night, motoring when the wind dropped in the evening.

Nigel's heart yearned southward ahead of *Sandalshoon's* hurrying bows, to Nicola, who had said on the crackling and buzzing radio that she loved him and would marry him.

Campanida made ninety miles the second day, and on the third came in the evening, in a dying wind, to the rendezvous.

This was a small island, twenty miles north-west of St Lucia – dry, uninhabited, useless, flat and dull.

Another yacht was already there, anchored thirty yards off the inhospitable shore. A small figure waved madly from the foredeck. Colly recognised Jenny and gave a shout of joy and greeting.

Colly anchored and they started to lower the sails. Jenny came across in *Sandalshoon's* tender. She and Colly embraced warmly. She kissed Nicola, who wept.

'I thought you'd rather meet Nigel in our house, love.'

'Yes,' said Nicola.

Nigel appeared on *Sandalshoon's* deck, looking red-brown and different and grown-up. He helped Nicola aboard and she clung to him and would not thereafter let go of his hand.

Sandro went across to *Campanula*. He helped Colly with his sails and his prisoners. He heard Colly's report, and brought him up to date with what they had learnt.

'It comes to this,' said Colly finally. 'We don't know if the thing can continue to run on its own momentum. He may have the blackmail end set up so that his clients have to go on paying, even though he's at the bottom of this ocean.'

'I think he must be there. He was going to New York for a few days, for business. We believe for some pay-offs. I think the money comes to him quickly and he takes charge of it and turns it into yachts and property and investments, whatever he buys. The sums are exceedingly large, yes?'

'Matt's were.'

'There is a second thing we don't know,' said Sandro. 'Who is Mr Henry Body?'

'Huh?'

'A most civilised man, a man of culture, widely travelled, who does not exist.'

'Take it slow, Sandro. I'm tired.'

'I have been busy with *Sandalshoon's* very superior radio. Mr Body is legal owner of this and that and he has a passport. I repeat that he does not exist. He has no money, he lives nowhere, he exists only when he is here.'

'For God's sake, all you're saying is that he uses a different name in New York.'

'He is another person in New York, it is clear. Rich, well-known, with many connections. *But we do not know who.*'

'Does it matter?'

'*Molto.* This half man can hardly be arrested. If he is tried it will be for nothing. We shall not know the full story, the operation. Jenny will not be safe, nor any of us.'

'They'll take him to New York. Somebody will recognise him.'

'No. This man is full of confidence.'

'Let me go look at him.'

'Please do. I will stay here.'

Mr Henry Body looked back at Colly with arrogance.

'I may possibly be held to have committed a small number of minor technical offences. Who hasn't? To give you a representative example, I may unwittingly have travelled with a girl with a false name in her passport. That is the level we are discussing. A far cry from piracy.'

'What did George do with those other girls?'

'Since I understand that George was drowned his evidence in the matter will not be available to you.'

'What about the drugs in *Campanula?*'

'What drugs in *Campanula*? I guess we shall never know how George got them or why.'

'What about the drugs on board here?'

'You will find British prescriptions.'

'Abduction,' said Colly.

'Whom did I abduct?'

'Miss Nicola Bland.'

'I? From London? You will find from my passport that I have never even been to Britain.'

'We know beyond any doubt that you were in Britain.'

'My passport will conclusively prove different. You will discover, if you wish to take the trouble, that my legal domicile is in the British West Indies and that I have not been home to the United States for eight years.'

'You murdered six cops and a sucker at Rillington Beach, New Jersey.'

Henry Body laughed. 'My passport will conclusively prove different.'

Colly could make nothing of his face at all. But that head would be unforgettable. If pictures were circulated someone would remember.

Colly instructed his imagination to invest Henry Body with a head of hair. Various heads of hair. It meant nothing. And it was still a tiny head.

'I expect he has some sort of stuffed wig,' said Nicola, her voice muffled against Nigel's shoulder. 'To make his head bigger.'

Nigel exclaimed sharply: 'Sandro!'

'Yes? Dinner is nearly ready.'

'In New York he has a large head! An exceptionally big head . . . '

'Clever Nicola,' said Sandro.

When they knew what they were looking for they found it quite easily, though it was ingeniously camouflaged.

It was neatly packed in a leather zip-bag. This bore, in letters of gold, the words: 'LAPLANDERS. Travelling slippers by Keppels of Boston. Imported.' Inside the bag were what seemed to be a pair of shaggy folding slippers. One of these unfolded into a sort of flexible crash-helmet, covered with thick grey hair.

Sandro, searching earlier, had wondered momentarily at this cold-weather item amidst Henry Body's elegant tropical kit.

Sandro came into the saloon carrying the false head. A look of death came into Henry Body's face when he saw it. He struggled like a madman when they put it on him. Nicola came in, and saw it, and looked about for Henry Body. It was as though he had been given an entirely new head, a personality entirely remote.

Joins were faintly visible between eyebrows and ears. Glasses would exactly cover these. Sandro found the glasses, heavy-framed tortoiseshell of an intellectual kind, in a drawer. He put them on Henry Body's nose.

Colly came aboard to look.

'My God,' he said at the third attempt. He turned to Sandro. 'You were right, chum. The culture and all that. Remember Sotheby's?'

'Yes,' said Sandro. 'The purchaser of the large Matisse, property of the late Matt Warren.'

'Now that,' said Jenny, 'I call slick. Not just bleeding the poor bleeder to death, but publicly snapping up his household Gods.'

'Yeah,' said Colly. 'Goddam psychopath.'

'I wonder if that explains his taste in girls?'

'Revenge for being laughed at by a British chick the year

of Roosevelt's second term? But he's awful smart for a nut, darling.'

'No wonder,' said Nigel, 'they made such a fuss about the slipper in the car.'

'I think you were in a hurry that evening, Mr Body,' said Sandro. 'I think you changed your identity at short notice, perhaps in the car, when your friends spotted Miss Bland.'

'Wait,' said Jenny. 'It's two men, is it? Two quite different men. Tiny-head mucks about down here. Then a chum of his who's been staying with him flies to America and smooths about New York.'

'A man with a big head. Right. Tiny-head never goes near New York. And big-head,' said Colly, 'big-head, with a different passport, flies to Europe and buys pictures at Sotheby's.'

'But when he's talking to his London pals he's a man with a tiny head.'

'Yep. A man who never even entered the country. A man who can't be linked to anything.'

'And when,' said Nigel, 'he's roasting policemen—'

'He has a tiny head. A guy who never entered the United States, who never left Antigua. While the big-headed party has never been seen in New Jersey.'

'How mixed I'm getting,' said Jenny.

'That is the beauty,' said Sandro. 'Mr Body, by himself, as he has so often pointed out, has done very little that is criminal. Since he has been neither to Europe nor to the United States. And the gentleman with the large head even less. Only when you add them together . . . '

'Man,' said Colly, 'a change of heads is certainly convenient.'

The man with the large head, the thatch of grey hair, the neat features, and the great wealth stared at Jenny, at Sandro, at Colly, at Nigel and Nicola as though at the face of his personal damnation.

'How did we get here?' asked Nicola suddenly.

'You seem to have come as a naked Negress, darling,' said

Nigel.

'Oh,' she seemed taken aback. 'How sweet.'

They decided to assemble everybody in *Sandalshoon,* where there was plenty of room. Lyn and Albie the photographer were ferried across. Chuck, Ricky, Lyn and Albie were tied up in the forecastle. Colly brought a few of his own things across. He and Sandro would sleep on *Sandalshoon's* deck.

Mr Henry Body watched these dispositions in silence, his eyes flickering from left to right as he saw friends and enemies finally assembled in one hull.

'How dramatically correct,' he said at last. 'Stars and full company for the finale.' A note of exultation entered his voice as he said: 'It will not in the event be of any use to you, but it is an indulgence which, like Siegfried, I cannot deny myself.'

'What's that?' said Colly shortly.

'You postulated a British girl rejecting me. You were grotesquely short of the truth. I went to school in England. At the deplorable whim of my mother I was sent to a bad and minor boarding-school in the English Midlands. I was not happy there.'

Jenny imagined it: a clever and arrogant outsider with an unattractive deformity, among the oafish sons of builders and seed-merchants. He must have had a beastly time.

'I spent vacations with English families,' Mr Body went on softly. 'Families who were paid to take me, so that my mother could drink and drug and copulate in New York without interference. I was attracted to the English girls, the sisters of my schoolmates. They treated me with disgust and derision. On one occasion I was defiled. Stripped and defiled, by a group of girls. They laughed when I cried with shame and disgust. One of the girls was the daughter of a Minister of the Established Church. She was evil and obscene. She had an educated voice. I made a vow.'

'You kept it,' said Jenny.

There was still a note of exultation in Henry Body's soft and cultured voice as he went on: 'When I came home I found my mother had been ruined. In health and in spirit and financially, by the men who had used her. Hard, uncaring, selfish men, gentlemen, the Eastern Establishment, men who laughed at me when they were drunk in their clubs, for deformity and for poverty and for being the son of my mother. I made another vow.'

'You kept it,' said Colly.

'I wanted three things. My brilliance and my good fortune were that I killed all my birds with the same bright stone. I became richer than those men, my enemies. I reduced girls like the girls who had humiliated me to a degradation lower than a West Side hooker, lower than a Bowery bum, lower than my mother. I destroyed men like the men who had ruined my mother. Drove them to despair and to suicide, as she was driven. Yes, I kept my vows. I succeeded. Nobody can take it away from me.'

He was almost singing. His voice rose in a mad and priestlike incantation.

'You cannot undo what I have done. You cannot recall those men back to life and happiness, those girls back to decency. I have kept my vows. I have won.'

'Not this round,' said Colly. 'Let's get him somewhere we don't have to look at him.'

'You know,' said Jenny quietly to Sandro and Colly, after dinner, on *Sandalshoon's* afterdeck, 'I think it would be very nice and tactful for us three to go back to *Campanula*.'

'Aha, oho,' said Colly.

'Why not?' said Sandro. 'Mr Body is safe in the galley, the rest forward. Why not?'

Quietly they rowed across the strip of water between the yachts. When Nigel and Nicola came up on deck from the saloon they could see the tender at *Campanula's* stern; they could see Jenny wave from the bows.

Except for a living cargo who were not in a position to interrupt them, they were alone.

The wind had dropped and the sea was quiet. Nigel led Nicola below to the after cabin. He locked the door, pointlessly. Moonlight flooded in through the porthole.

They kissed with wide-open mouths. Nigel gently unbuttoned Nicola's shirt, and then pulled off his own. Body met body. Nicola squirmed with joy and strained towards Nigel. They lowered themselves slowly on to the moonlit double bunk. They undressed each other and explored each other's bodies. They made love in the moonlight.

Nicola slept for a little in Nigel's arms. She woke and said she wanted to swim.

He laughed and kissed her. They went up on deck as they were. Nicola climbed down the ladder into the sea. Nigel dived from the deck. They kissed again in the water, body to body. They wondered if they could make love while they were swimming. They let themselves drift a little way from the yacht. This saved their lives.

Finale

The explosion seemed to start quite slowly, in the forward part of *Sandalshoon*. There was a brief orange glow, then an appalling crack. The yacht's forward coachwork mushroomed outwards and a pale cloud of flame bloomed over the quiet sea. Flames ran aft and there was another explosion. Burning diesel oil showered the water. In the glare of the fire the moon disappeared.

'My God,' said Sandro, choking. 'The lovers.'

Jenny, on the afterdeck of *Campanula,* pointed at the water. They could see two dark heads against the blaze. Within seconds Colly was in the tender picking them up.

'Whenever we meet,' said Nicola to Colly as Nigel pulled her into the Boston dory, 'I'm flopping about in the water with nothing on.'

Colly got them well away from the magnificent holocaust. They sat looking at it.

'Nothing we can do,' called Sandro.

Nigel and Nicola climbed self-consciously aboard *Campanula* and were wrapped in towels. The five of them stared awestruck across the lurid water.

'I don't say you two were *wrong:* said Jenny to Nigel finally. 'In fact, I daresay you were right. But I do think, pet, you should have consulted us.'

'Christ, you don't think we started it?'

'What do you expect us to think?'

'It started forward,' said Colly. 'I guess the galley. The calorgas cylinders.'

'How?'

'Mr Body. I guess with his foot. Then he'd use the automatic lighter. There is one? Electric?'

'Yes,' said Nigel. 'Works from a battery.'

'With his *foot*, Colly?'

'We'll never know. He had an hour. What a way to die.'

'A Viking funeral,' said Nigel.

Nicola shivered and snuggled against him. There was no trace in her now of the smart, self-conscious London copywriter; nor of the animated corpse who had to be pushed through doors. There was no trace in Nigel now of the charcoal-grey-suited executive-on-his-way-up.

They could feel the heat of the burning yacht, though *Campanula* was well out of reach of danger.

'A Viking funeral,' repeated Sandro. 'And he took his retinue with him to Valhalla.'

'And you two,' said Jenny, 'you two just decided to go for a dip?'

'Yes,' said Nicola.

'Good gracious.'

'Of course,' said Colly, 'he thought we were all on board.'

'So he did,' said Jenny faintly. 'Which but for being arch and sentimental . . . Gracious. What a moral there is there.'

The thick metal masts thudded down almost together, landing in great showers of sparks. Much of *Sandalshoon* was metal; much was also wood, plastic, paint, fabric. The five sat watching for a long time.

'Would they be killed instantly?' asked Nicola.

'Body, yes, just about,' said Colly, 'leaving aside the time he took starting it. The blast might have knocked the others out. Or maybe not.'

'I feel a bit sorry,' said Jenny, 'for Chuck Running Deer. And little Albie Joy. I suppose that's silly.'

'Quite silly,' said Sandro.

'All of a sudden I horribly want a drink. I suppose that's silly too.'

'Most sensible.'

Bad Bet

Mathew Carver is a successful Kentucky bloodstock breeder and racehorse owner with a considerable reputation. He is also a member of a syndicate consisting of men significantly richer than himself. Through him the reader is immersed in the world of racing from bloodstock sales at Newmarket, to the classic countryside of Normandy, the Bluegrass of Kentucky and the mansions of Virginia. Racing's aristocracy and its hard men, the touts, the fraudsters, the stable lads, tipsters and jockeys all provide the action and the sometime dubious underlying morality associated with the many sub-plots that develop. And Mathew himself is pulled in many different directions, not least by the three women in his life, two of whom love him and his wife who hates him. There is an extraordinary array of characters involved, and Longrigg's deep knowledge of racing is apparent as he weaves together the passion, disasters, hopes, triumphs, tragedies and humorous interludes that befall them.

Albany

Leonora Albany's great-grandmother harboured an astonishing secret. It seems that Leonora is the sole legitimate descendant of Bonnie Prince Charlie – and by rights, the Queen of Scotland. The seventeen-year old's pursuit of truth leads her to a path strewn with danger, violence and an unspeakable murder. Laura Black brings to life the struggles of an extraordinary adolescent in her fight to remain unconsumed by title and privilege. Mystery and suspense surround every character in this spellbinding tale of intrigue.

Praying Mantis

Victoria Courtenay is beautiful, charming to the core, although this is almost wholly affectation as she has an underlying ruthlessness in which she uses her looks and manner to obtain whatever she wants. Indeed, it goes much further as she has a thoroughly evil streak which drives her to lure people in and then strike, as a praying mantis. She is determined to get her way, with family, friends, and lovers ... This novel is one of psychological suspense at its best and is full of surprises.

Necklace Of Skulls

Lady Jennifer Norrington, Colly and Sandro travel to India to uncover a drug-stealing operation which develops into something altogether more horrible and frightening. Jenny is caught and used as bait for the others by the perpetrators of a long series of religious murders that was thought to have been stamped out in the nineteenth century, but as an organisation still survives. This wholly credible tale is set against exotic backgrounds and contains the kind of detail readers have come to expect of Drummond. It is a true suspense novel in all of the best traditions, with plot and sub-plots and many surprises.

Paper Boats

The proceeds of a wage robbery come, by mistake, into the hands of Gregory Pratt as he sits on his commuter train. Gregory lives, with his father, in deprived circumstances in an old mansion which is converted into a form of commune for distressed gentlefolk. Gregory struggles with his conscience over the money, but his father is certain; no one will suffer if they apply the find to their own purposes, and those of their neighbours. This is a story of high comedy, shrewd observation, and an exciting read from cover to cover.

Snare In The Dark

Dan Mallett usually keeps one step in front of the police and authority in the west- country village where he lives. Dan goes out one night to poach pheasants, and it is on that night that Major March's gamekeeper is shot dead with an arrow. Knowing he will almost automatically be blamed, he disappears whilst devising a plan to identify the real villain.

Roger Longrigg was a British author of unusual versatility who wrote both novels and non-fiction, along with plays and screenplays for television, under both his own name and eight other pseudonyms, including *Laura Black, Ivor Drummond, Domini Taylor,* and *Frank Parish.*

Born in Edinburgh into a military family, he was at first schooled in the Middle East, but returned to England as a youth and later read history at Magdalen College, Oxford. His early career took him into advertising, but after the publication of two comic novels he took up writing full time in 1959.

He completed fifty five books, many under his own name, but also Scottish historical fiction as *Laura Black*; thrillers as *Ivor Drummond*; black comedies as *Domini Taylor*; and famously *Rosalind Erskine* – a name with which he hoaxed all for several years – who appeared to write a disguised biography of what life was like in a girls boarding school where, with classmates, she ran a brothel for boys from a nearby school. 'The Passion Flower Hotel' became a bestseller and was later filmed.

Roger Longrigg's work in television included '*Mother Love*', a BBC mini-series starring Diana Rigg and David McCallum, and episodes of '*Crown Court*' and '*Dial M for Murder*'. He died in 2000, aged 70, and was survived by his wife, the novelist Jane Chichester, and three daughters.

C333871940

Works by Roger Longrigg
Published by House of Stratus

BABE IN THE WOOD
BAD BET
DAUGHTERS OF MULBERRY
THE DESPERATE CRIMINALS
A HIGH PITCHED BUZZ
THE JEVINGTON SYSTEM
LOVE AMONG THE BOTTLES
THE PAPER BOATS
THE SUN ON THE WATER
SWITCHBOARD
THEIR PLEASING SPORT
WRONG NUMBER

AS LAURA BLACK:
ALBANY
CASTLE RAVEN
FALLS OF GARD
GLENDRACO
STRATHGALLANT

AS IVOR DRUMMOND:
THE DIAMONDS OF LORETA
THE FROG IN THE MOONFLOWER
THE JAWS OF THE WATCHDOG
THE MAN WITH THE TINY HEAD
THE NECKLACE OF SKULLS
THE POWER OF THE BUG
THE PRIESTS OF THE ABOMINATION
THE STENCH OF POPPIES
THE TANK OF SACRED EELS

AS FRANK PARISH:
BAIT ON THE HOOK
CAUGHT IN THE BIRDLIME
FACE AT THE WINDOW
FIRE IN THE BARLEY
FLY IN THE COBWEB
SNARE IN THE DARK
STING OF THE HONEYBEE

AS DOMINI TAYLOR:
THE EYE BEHIND THE CURTAIN
GEMINI
MOTHER LOVE
NOT FAIR
PRAYING MANTIS
SIEGE
SUFFER LITTLE CHILDREN
THE TIFFANY LAMP